AF425022

The Ranger

A Western Novel

Richard G. Hole

Far West 3

El Paso was the ideal city for many strange things due to its proximity to the Mexican border, to which by tradition they sent the undesirable weapons for the revolutionary guerrillas and cattle to feed these guerrillas.

The smuggling of arms and cattle across the border was highly appreciated by the enemies of Emperor Maximilian, imposed by the French on the throne of Mexico and wanted to overthrow by the supporters of Juarez, and the necessary money did not it mattered when it came to providing the elements most necessary to keep the revolution and the struggle alive.

The Ranger is a story belonging to the Far West collection, a collection of novels developed in the American Wild West.

THE RANGER

Chapter I

RANGER VOCATION

Harry Parker, at the end of the Civil War, found himself with a shiny license in his pocket, a pair of well-earned medals, three scars hidden under the worn warrior, some sergeant's badges that had no value anymore, and about fifty dollars for capital. All this testimony to a very glorious and emotional past, but nothing valuable for a very uncertain future.

Because the war had left several states unhinged, including Texas, which although geographically did not suffer painful scars if it was accused in the chaos and disorganization of daily life.

Many ranches had disappeared, others were abandoned as dilapidated, the cattle ran out or dispersed without anyone to take care of them due to the lack of men mired in the conflict and if this was not enough, banditry, plundering action, the parties of the soulless united in gangs to possess a greater force of aggression, they were dominating almost the entire immense state.

Harry thought about his future. The logical thing was to go back to his own thing, to the horse and the rope, to look for a ranch where to settle to resume a life of work cut short by the war, but this, apart from the fact that it was not easy at the moment, seemed not to please him fully, now that he had His life course changed and from a peaceful cowboy he had become a formidable fighter.

Without knowing why, he had taken a liking to fighting, he was seduced by the dangerous emotion of the fight, the uncertainty of what might happen, the excitement produced by knowing that there was a nearby enemy with whom he had to contend and sharpen his wits. , control your nerves and sharpen your aim to be victorious. All of this had gotten into his young blood like a poisonous virus, and he was rebelling to give it up in order to plunge back into the monotonous and vulgar life of the pastures.

But the war was over and that emotion was reserved for those who were outside the law. Only they could continue to face the danger, but in an anonymous, creeping way, without a noble purpose and with the exposure not of dying in a legal fight in the sunlight, but hanging from a rope.

And this was not what he longed for. He had been born honorable, he had fought under the sign of an honorable flag, and he could not disgrace it after the war. He was not born to be a cattle rustler or a robber, and he could not hurl himself down those paths that he fiercely repudiated.

But instead, he did believe he had been born for something more noble after his painful experience of war. The man who had given so many tests of courage, audacity and mettle during the war, was hardened for danger and could well constitute an excellent ranger, much more, in those moments when the explosion of banditry demanded an increase in strength in the field. Corps to be able to impose law and order and to sweep the rapacious hordes from the meadows and mountains that threatened to make the situation of the State even more painful and serious.

This did please him, it would be a continuation of what he had just left, although in a different order. An open fight without quarter with a more despicable enemy, because they did not fight more or less mistakenly for a cause and under the flag of a flag, but they killed for selfishness, profit and the desire to kill.

Being a ranger was all his illusion. At the end of his twenty-six years, he believed that he had now discovered his true vocation and his longing made it the golden dream of the future, but he did not see very clearly the possibility of being admitted to the Corps.

In those moments when Confucianism reigned and no one knew exactly who was who, the commanders of the famous and brave Corps acted with enormous caution. They needed rangers, but they were careful not to admit more than men with a solid moral guarantee, since, if they did not act with this prudence, they were liable to bring into their ranks lazy, drunk, undesirables, people who under the cover of the glorious gray uniform of each Division could not only dishonor its immaculate record, but sow in it the poison of many devastating things.

And he was a complete stranger with no solid endorsement to submit with an application. He knew it would be a waste of time trying and he was not here to waste it, when his financial situation was precarious. He would have to give up such a beautiful dream and wander the prairie in search of some possible ranch where he could go back to handling the lasso meekly, although he did not consider it easy.

The morning that he was going to leave his old regiment to get away from the war environment, before leaving, he looked for his captain to say goodbye to him.

The captain was a brave man. He had risen from lieutenant almost on the same battlefield and Harry fought alongside him in many actions, being one of his most trusted men. When he presented himself to say goodbye, the captain asked:

"Well boy, this is over. Where will you go and what will you do now?

"That's what I, my captain, was asking myself. Things, according to my news, are not very clear in Texas and it seems that the whole issue of livestock is a mess that will take time to fix. I do not know if I will find where to act again, or I will have to move to California or Arizona, where things will be a little more in order. My pleasure would have been to be able to apply for a place in the rangers now that many more are going to be needed to guarantee the law, but I know that this is very difficult because there is a lot of expungement among applicants and only those who can present a good endorsement are admitted. You will tell me that my service record is already a solid guarantee, but I do not think it is worth it, because there are guys that the war forced them to be brave by instinct and now that bravery will be used very badly.

The captain stared at him and asked:

"Would you really like to join the rangers?

"Of course you do, my captain; It's my golden dream I think that now that I have overcome fear, that I have fired, that I am in the environment and I do not attach great importance to danger because I learned to tame it many times, I could play a good role in the Corps. I am young, I am healthy, I am not a coward and I have great stamina. If I could carry a guarantee of morality attached to these conditions, I think I would be admitted and if it were, I am sure that they would not regret admitting me to any division.

The captain, smiling, replied:

Think about it, boy. You have cheated death many times, why go on defying it unnecessarily?

"I don't know, it will be because I made fun of her and I am not afraid of her.

"In that case, I will try to help you. The captain of Division K who has his mission in "El Paso" is a friend of mine; If you haven't changed your Body and you are still there, I hope you will take care of me because you know me well and you know that I would not recommend a bad apple. I'll give you a letter for him and you will introduce yourself. Then, I no longer answer that it has all the effect that you intend, but I can not do more.

"And it is too much, my captain," Harry affirmed enthusiastically. Being his friend and knowing him, you will be sure that he does not deceive you anymore ... because I am lucky to be admitted right away. It would be something that neither dreamed of.

"Well, get your things ready and go back for the letter.

Harry, mad with joy, packed his old little suitcase with the clothes and trifles it contained and a little later, he presented himself again to the captain. A strange fever dominated him and when he closed his eyes pondering the future, he saw himself on horseback wearing the honorable uniform of the beaters and chasing across the landscape the gangs of robbers and murderers who began to carry out their pernicious activities in the South and West. from Texas.

The captain had already written the letter. It was brief, but expressive and highly complimentary, so much so that the boy blushed when he read what it said about her courage, her loyalty, and her morality.

Here you go. I am convinced that if there is a chance that you will be admitted, you will be welcomed.

"Thank you very much, my captain. If so, you will make me the happiest man on earth.

"Or the most unfortunate, Harry. You still don't know what the hard life of the rangers is and the dangers they run. They earn excessively what they charge and for them there is no other life than mobility, persecution, danger, suffering cold, snow, mud, water, sun, fatigue, hardships and dangers. Good luck and go as far in that uniform as you have come in this one.

"Thank you. I will try to leave him in the place he deserves.

And putting the letter away, she said goodbye to him with an emotional handshake.

Harry made his way to "El Paso" by the fastest means he could find, which were not many, because the transports were as disjointed as life in the nation and one day, after a long and very heavy journey, he would arrive in the city borderline and anger with a heart overflowing with enthusiasm, but at the same time, with the fear of suffering the greatest disappointment of his life.

The city was abuzz with people. The end of the war imposed a great dynamism to reorganize life in all sectors. The people, aggressive and optimistic, were preparing to start businesses, to reestablish commerce, to do something to heal the wounds of war and alleviate the hunger and ruin that devastated many sectors and many homes.

Some worn uniforms of the first graduates were also seen circulating through the streets, who in turn sought accommodation in their previous activities or in those that the need imposed on them. They were not lacking among them strange-looking men, people who seemed to denounce to the mile that it was not decent work they were looking for precisely. El Paso was the ideal city for many strange things due to its proximity to the Mexican border, to which by tradition they sent the undesirable weapons for the revolutionary guerrillas and cattle to feed these guerrillas.

The smuggling of arms and cattle across the border was highly appreciated by the enemies of Emperor Maximilian, imposed by the French on the throne of Mexico and wanted to overthrow by the supporters of Juarez, and the necessary money did not it mattered when it came to providing the elements most necessary to keep the revolution and the struggle alive.

This was known to all the border dwellers and although the United States Government did not want to get involved in the lawsuit and tried to cut off any intervention in favor of one or the other, its power in such unhinged moments did not extend to control everything. the course of the Rio Grande and avoid that illegal traffic that if it produced disasters in the Mexicans, because it helped to maintain the warlike state, it also harmed the United States, because both the cattle and the weapons, was a dispossession that was done to the ranchers, and even the nation's own weapons depots.

Harry, who had already lost his vision of what was a peaceful town, albeit noisy and gruff, seemed to feel displaced in its streets. The instinct of the danger he had been in for so long made him distrustful and, without realizing it, he looked right and left or up and down, believing that at any moment the unknown danger would arise.

Finally, after asking, he located the Ranger barracks. An unusual movement was observed in it, men came and went, some in civilian clothes, others wearing military uniforms or some garment of it and everything seemed to indicate that the movement of men was overwhelming and uncontrollable.

Two Rangers with a weary look at the parade stood guard at the gate. Harry approached one, asking:

"Captain Walter, will you please?

"Captain Walter? Oh, the captain is fuming, bachelor! They do not leave him in the sun or shade, he has received more than a hundred applicants and I do not think he is in a very good mood. If it's a question of asking for a place in the Division, you'd better resign. He is tired of firing people, telling them that the quota is filled.

The answer was not very comforting to Harry, but he must not resign without a fight and he replied:

"I have a letter for him, from a captain who has been at the front and is a close friend of his.

"Hmm! Well, that's another thing ... Job, accompany the friend to the captain's office and tell him what there is.

The sentry guided Harry through the corridors and stairs and led him upstairs, where Captain Walter had his office. He could be heard shouting from half a dozen men in his office.

"I tell you I'm sorry, but it can't be here. Go to San Antonio or Vacco, where you may need men. Here everything is covered "and nervously pushed them to make them leave the office.

The group disappeared and the captain, snorting, faced the ranger:

"What happens now, Job?

"My captain, this ex-combatant says he brought a letter from a friend of yours from the front line. That is why I have let him pass.

"Okay, Job, let him.

And pointing to the door, he indicated:

"Come in, Sergeant.

Harry walked in excited. He felt the fear of that trip in vain and could not hide the anguish that it caused him.

The captain, taking the letter that the lawyer presented him, asked:

"Where do you come from, Sergeant?

"From New Orleans.

"Good site. Were you there during the taking of the city?

"Yes my captain. I was in the capture of the fort of San Carlos and later I entered the city with the rest of the troops.

"You beat the copper well there, didn't you?

"Well yes, my captain. It was quite "hot" and some got burned. Others were lucky.

The captain took the letter and the first thing he looked for was the signature. Deciphering it, he smiled with pleasure.

"Wow, it's from Gray! Have you fought under his command?

"Almost three years, my captain. Since he was a lieutenant.

"Good boy and bravo. It will go far.

There were a few minutes of silence while I read the contents of the letter. When he finished, he put it on the table, commenting:

"Gray raves about you, do you deserve it?

"I don't know, my captain, but he knows that I have tried to deserve them.

"Excellent reply, Sergeant. This is how men should be. As you tell me here, your name is Harry Parker.

"Yes sir.

"Where were you born?

"Here in Texas, in a town near Corpus Christi Bay.

"Were you a cowboy?

"Yes, but my boss's ranch was razed by the southern guerrillas and his cattle disappeared. There was no way to get back to him.

"I understand. From what I see, you have won two medals in action of war.

"At least they granted them to me. I also got three scars that I don't wear because they are uglier than medals.

The captain smiled; he was amused by the childish humor of the graduate.

"Well, and with all that baggage and the recommendation of my friend, you come to apply to be admitted to the rangers.

"Yes my captain. If I had not had that recommendation, I would not have dared, because they had told me that it was very difficult and, furthermore, in order to avoid admitting people of doubtful condition, only those who presented a solid guarantee were served. He offered it to me and I thanked him very much, although ... his good wish is nothing, because I have already seen how dozens come to request the same.

"That's right, Sergeant, but they're not all the same. Have you ever thought that even if you were admitted, your army graduation would be of no use to you? Here promotions are earned on merit in service to the Corps.

"I do not care about that. In the army they promoted me without me looking for him; here, if I managed to get in, I'd be careful to win them over. I don't know, maybe I'm wrong, maybe I'll fail, I may not be one of many if I get to wear the uniform, but if I do wear it, I'll put all my soul and everything I have to put into earning those promotions that I would give to my former captain. in payment to your recommendation. I have the evidence that I was born to ranger and would like to test whether it is true or not.

"Well, after giving you those warnings, I can tell you that, of the few places reserved for unavoidable commitments, I can offer one as a gift to my friend Gray. I know that he would serve me the same in something that I asked him and I know that he would not recommend you if he was not sure that you will leave him well.

"So I... can count on... being admitted to the Corps and...

"Am I not telling you? You are admitted and we will test if it is true how you think you were born to ranger. There are many delicate things to take care of, I need enough men of mettle for certain risky and hard services and since you consider yourself valid for them, I will try you on some that will give me the measure of your ability. The promotions are there, in those services and you will have the same probability as others to earn them.

"Thank you very much, my captain," Harry exclaimed with a trembling voice, "you do not know how happy you make me with this concession and I solemnly promise you that I will go as far as the most, I will do what the most and where the most is exposed. I will expose myself first. If you ever meet my former captain and talk to him about me, I want it to be to affirm that I was able to honor his recommendation and that I am the best.

"Well, nothing more Harry. For today you are free to rest from the trip and tomorrow morning, at nine o'clock, come to have your affiliation taken and included on the list.

"Thank you very much, Captain Walter. Tomorrow at nine o'clock you will have me here.

He saluted stiffly and left the office with his heart leaping for joy. The dream that he had been cherishing and that he already believed was impossible, had just come true thanks to a simple letter, but that letter contained all his patriotic spirit, his courage, his honesty and his efficiency.

Starting tomorrow, he would be a ranger, proudly wearing the gray scouts' uniform, and preparing to prove himself in the line of duty.

Joyful he looked for an inn to sleep that night and took advantage of the day to tour the city.

Chapter II

A GREAT VISIT

The next day at the appointed time, Harry was in the barracks waiting for the moment to be filmed and included in the lists of the Division.

He was not the only one who was waiting for admission, with him was a tall, blond, lanky boy, with very blue eyes and curly hair. He seemed to come from Irish parents judging by his type.

He was also a graduate, although because of the warrior he still wore, he had not passed from a simple soldier. The young man looked at Harry with some respect as he discovered the sergeant's insignia on his tunic. Military discipline was still ingrained in him and he mechanically rose to his feet as Harry entered, but Harry, with an imperative gesture, ordered:

"Sit down, will you please. Here I am neither more nor less than anyone and if I still wear these badges it is not because of vanity, but because I did not have other clothes to change. Anyway, soon I will change it for another simpler and less showy, although no less honorable for that. I will be one more number in the Corps and no one will have to remember that I was something in the Army of the North.

"Have you been admitted to the Rangers?

"So it seems, do you?

"Also. It seems that of as many as we went yesterday to try to enlist, only you and I have had this luck.

"Indeed. I stay thanks to the spirited recommendation of the captain of my company, with whom I fought for three years. If not for him, I would not have been admitted.

"Yes, it is very difficult. I have a job because I am the brother of Sergeant Bob Reggs. My name is Caro Reggs.

"Me, Harry Parker.

"I am glad to meet you, Sergeant, and I hope that if we are assigned to the same company, we will be good friends and colleagues. My brother is a veteran of the Rangers and is highly appreciated in the Corps. I would have entered it sooner if the war had not broken out, but when it did break out, my brother told me that I would earn more by enlisting first in the army, where I would learn and acquire practice and toughness. It does not weigh me down, because in reality I have gotten rid of a hard learning.

"Yes; war teaches a lot and shows us if we are worth later for something similar. You are a Texan too.

"Not doubt about it. We were born near Austin, but when my brother was promoted to sergeant and was permanently in this Division, Bob decided that we all come here. My mother, my sister Cynthia and me. We sold our small property and bought a piece of land on the outskirts of El Paso, where we have a very acceptable cabin and some land. Thus, my brother was able to take care of the family as much as possible and when he does not have service, he spends some time with my mother and my sister.

»My mother is somewhat sorry because she is always afraid that something might happen to my brother and now to me. In no way did he want me to join, also in the rangers, but what better thing am I going to find now as everything is unhinged? Here you earn a decent salary, you have a safe food and you can help the family. My brother has suffered this burden for a long time, but now I can help him bear it, and between the two of us, ours will not suffer fatigue or deprivation. Do you have the family far away?

"Just a few second-degree relatives.

"That is worse; family is always a comfort and a refuge.

"True, but when something like this is chosen, which is dangerous, the family suffers thinking about one's luck and one suffers thinking about them. You know it.

"It's true; everything has its pros and cons.

The presence of Captain Walter cut off the dialogue. They both stood up saluting militarily.

"Hello, guys" greeted the captain in turn. Right now they will take your affiliation and the requirements for your entry will be met. Reggs, I have ordered that once everything is in order, you are added to the company your brother commands. He is very interested in guiding your first steps and since I have something important for him to entrust to him, I, in turn, want him to take you to his side and test you in the blank. Bob is too rigid to overlook anything he doesn't like and even if you are his brother he wouldn't bite his tongue in giving me the report.

"Thank you very much, Captain Walter," Caro replied firmly. " My brother will have no opportunity to misrepresent me.

"I'll celebrate... Well guys, I let you guys have a lot to do.

A ranger went up in search of the couple to take them to the offices, where after taking their affiliation they were assigned their position, they were told what their duffel bags were in the bedrooms and they were taken to the warehouse to have their uniforms delivered.

An hour later, they were both excitedly wearing the brand new gray uniforms and had in their possession the rifle, the revolver, both bearing the Corps anagram, the traveling bag and later, the horses they had to ride.

Harry really liked his. It was a magnificent specimen black as night, with an intelligent head and a hard skeleton, capable of enduring many exhausting days.

Later, they saw the captain again, who, smiling, commented:

"Well guys, you have already achieved your golden dream; now you just need to make yourself worthy of it.

"We can't wait to prove it," said Harry.

"Well, maybe it won't take you long. Now Bob will come to take care of you and since there will be nothing organized until tomorrow and because of your quality as ex-combatants you do not need prior instruction, this afternoon you can walk around the city a bit. Tomorrow will be another day.

He walked away from them and shortly after, Sergeant Bob Reggs appeared.

Harry liked her appearance. He was an impressive big man, who, although facially he looked a lot like his brother, humanly he disagreed with everything, since his height was much higher and his weight exceeded his brother by forty pounds.

He was a very dark man, with rough skin from the brutal caress of the elements and his skeleton must have been the hardness of rock.

But despite his severe gesture as a good military man, there was something attractive about his face, perhaps the soft glow of his blue eyes, perhaps the initiation of a natural half-smile that he could hide because it seemed congenital in him, something that Harry liked. in extreme.

Bob stepped forward, saying:

"Are you the new Ranger Harry Parker?

"At your command, my sergeant.

"I think you were in the army.

"Indeed, I was.

"And the captain has told me that he has some medals and some scars.

"That's right, my sergeant.

"Well, the medals, you can continue to wear them, even if the sergeant's stripes are of no use to you here. However, they can be rescued with good will.

"We will try to do it.

"Well, I have nothing to say to you. The captain recommends it to me with interest and I hope that neither you have a complaint about me, nor I about you. I like that men love me, but I also like that they know how to make themselves loved.

"As for you," he added, pointing to his brother, "forget about our relationship during acts of service, because when it comes to acting, for me you will be nothing more than a ranger from my company and I will be her sergeant for you.

«I think it is preferable to clarify the situation; otherwise, you can ask to be transferred to another.

"Okay Bob, I'll keep it in mind.

"Well, there is nothing more to talk about. You can have today and tomorrow you will start to act.

"In that case" said Caro ", I'm going to see mother and Cynthia to say goodbye to them and see how handsome I am in this uniform. I hope with your permission, Mr. Sergeant, that Mother and Cynthia find him more handsome than you.

"Okay, Caro, but you will give me greater joy if one day they think that you are braver than me too.

"That is no longer easy, Sergeant Reggs, but we will try.

The sergeant smiled and dismissed his brother with an affectionate pat on the back. Caro tugged on Harry's arm, saying:

"He is very rigid as a sergeant, but he has a child's heart and loves us all madly. Actually, he was the one who got us all forward.

Outside the barracks, Caro asked:

"What will you do now, Harry?

"I don't know, I don't have a preconceived plan.

"Why don't you walk me home? I will introduce you to my mother and sister and they will be happy to meet a good colleague of mine.

Harry nodded. Between being bored alone and accompanying Caro, this seemed more distracted.

Both went to the outskirts of the town on the eastern side. There, half a mile from the last houses, in the middle of the field, stood the cheerful and spacious Reggs cabin, surrounded by a large, well-tended orchard.

The hut, long and solid, had in the center a projecting covered porch with a wooden floor, protected by a kind of rough veranda made of thick interlaced branches.

On the sunny, happy morning a graceful female figure stood out on the porch. She hung clothes on a rope crossed from side to side of the porch and her position, raised on tiptoe to better encompass the rope, highlighted her with all the briosity of her beautiful, well-rounded body.

Caro recognized her instantly and noted:

"That's Cynthia, my sister.

And he whistled shrill in a peculiar way.

The young woman, catching the whistle, turned her body abruptly and looked towards the city. Upon discovering the two rangers advancing, he yelled:

"Mom, Mom, it's Caro coming!

And like a deer he ran fast to meet Caro.

The two hugged each other warmly and Harry stood to one side admiring the girl's soft, serene, yet dynamic and alluring beauty.

She was blonde like her brothers. She was more like Caro in body flexibility than Bob, and the ex-sergeant calculated that she should not exceed twenty-one years of age.

His eyes were intensely blue, but the poetic blue of a lake asleep under the caress of the sun. Her hair was naturally curly, forming graceful, loose loops. His nose was a bit upturned, which gave a mischievous and special grace to his face and he had a small and beautiful mouth, through whose lips when he smiled, he showed the double string of white, small and uniform teeth.

The girl, after embracing her brother effusively, separated a little and, examining him from top to bottom, commented:

"How handsome you are in the uniform, Caro! You are more handsome than Bob!

"Don't tell him, he's going to be offended.

"Bah! Bob is not offended by anything and less by that. You know that he loves us all very much.

At that moment, Martha, the Reggs' mother, appeared attracted by her daughter's call.

Seeing Caro in the ranger uniform, he stopped for a moment and exclaimed with some sadness:

"You finally made it, Caro. I will not forgive your brother for this ...

"But, Mom, the Rangers are doing very well and your life is assured. You know that times are bad to find something suitable and here ... well I can become a sergeant like my brother and earn a good salary.

"Yes, all that is fine if there were no thieves, smugglers and robbers to hunt down. It is not a dish to my liking having spent so much toil raising two children so that one day they will be shot at the edge of the river or in the mountains.

Come on, Mom, don't be pessimistic. Bob has been with the Rangers for four years and you see him, so alive and so healthy.

"What doesn't happen in four years happens in one day, Caro, and now the anxiety is double, because the danger is for both of us.

"Well, don't think about sad things now. Let me introduce you to a partner who will perform with me under Bob's orders.

This is Harry Parker, a former sergeant in the Northern Army during the war. He has won several medals for brave and has three scars on his body. You see, he was wounded three times and yet he lives.

And turning to Harry, he added:

"This is Martha, my mother, and this, Cynthia, my sister.

"Nice to meet you," said Harry, a little embarrassed, because Cynthia's suggestive beauty had impressed him and he was aware of the attraction of the young woman.

"The taste is ours," said Martha, "and I will be glad that you are good companions and get along well. You look like a more poised man and I hope you take care of this madman who does not care about anything. As for Bob, he is too serious, I admit, he has taken his mission as a priesthood and he is rigid as a rod of steel, but you see, at heart he is a boy disguised as a lion. When he takes the air you will win all his sympathy.

"I hope so, ma'am, and for my part, I will do my best to achieve it. If we are to live the same life of worries, jobs and dangers, it is only fair that we are so intertwined that we are one for all and all for one.

"God make it so. Now, I fear that things are much more arid than in these three years of war. While the war lasted, this has been relatively calm, there were many people on the fronts and here the businesses were poor, but with the discharge, according to Bob fears, many dangerous guys are going to overturn these lands with whom we will have to fight bitterly. to throw them out of here. This bloody border town is terrible, because it lends itself to a lot of dirty business and the theft and smuggling are feared to escalate. Tough days are ahead for you and this is my fear.

"The war was also hard and you had to fight daily; However, you see, your son, I and many more have weathered so many months of danger and have returned.

"I understand, but that does not save future dangers. Those have already passed, but what about those that remain?

"We will go over them with caution. We have experience and cold blood and that is worth a lot.

"God make your words confirm.

The old woman invited them to come in and sitting on the porch she served them mead that she had to refresh in the well.

Harry was glad he had accompanied Caro.

The presence of his attractive sister made him forget everything and he wished the day were endless to continue by her side.

While his mother interrogated his brother and gave him extensive and heavy advice that the boy listened to with a loving smile, Cynthia, curious to know things unknown, asked Harry about his campaign to take New Orleans, which had been reported. She spoke a lot even in those confines and she felt admired of the many lands that the former sergeant had traveled, of the various battles in which he had taken part and of the dangers that he had run when he fell wounded in the middle of the fight and was exposed to falling into hands of the Southerners.

Caro and her mother ended up disengaging from the couple. The boy had hinted at the idea of inviting his new companion to dinner to his mother, and the old woman had found the invitation quite natural.

And so Harry was invited to the simple family table and prolonged his coexistence with them for several hours, which for him were a quick dream.

Only at dusk, when Caro indicated that it was time to return to the barracks, did she realize how long she had been there and how short it had been. Cynthia, too, must have been cut short even though all day she barely did anything but chat with the ex-sergeant.

The farewell was cordial. Martha shook Harry's hand, pleading:

"You take care of my son, Mr. Harry. You inspire me a lot of confidence because you seem like a very seated man and Caro is a madman without poise. You say that this mission should be entrusted to your brother Bob, but Bob ... Bob is just a Ranger sergeant. You understand me?

Harry understood her. He wanted to imply that imbued with his graduation and duty, he sacrificed everything to its fulfillment, forgetting all sentimentality,

"I'll do my best, ma'am. Caro and I will be one and whatever belongs to one will belong to the other. As for Bob, don't judge him so harshly. Within the discipline there are many nuances and under a warrior always beats a heart from which one cannot coldly detach.

Cynthia's farewell was cordial. She simply said, shaking his hand:

"It has been a pleasure for us to meet you and I hope that when you return on duty and have some time off, you will visit us again. Here you will be received with all pleasure and affection.

"Thank you, Cynthia, I promise you that whenever there is an opportunity I will come to visit you and give you an account of our adventures. I hope that in the midst of their excitement everything goes well and smoothly.

The couple left the cabin to return to El Paso, but Harry felt so drawn to the Reggs' home that, without realizing it, every ten steps, he would turn his head, looking on the porch for the silhouette of Cynthia, who with a handkerchief in his hand waved them goodbye.

Chapter III

A DANGEROUS MISSION

Sergeant Bob Reggs had been locked in Captain Walter's office for over an hour exchanging impressions with him. The captain had something very important to make known to the sergeant and they had both been studying the case from every angle.

So that night, when Caro and Harry returned to the barracks,

Bob called both of them, saying:

"We are going to talk about something very important. The time has come to act and to put everyone's skills to the test.

Listen to me well, Harry. According to reports received by the captain, a well-known guy named Tymson Overman is in El Paso. It is a true reptile with oily skin capable of slipping out of the roughest hands and until now, it has managed to get no one to lay hands on it, accusing it of things that are in the minds of many.

»Tymson has operated a lot in this part of the international zone, but he has operated in the shadows, covering himself well so that no one has a vulnerable point against him; However, it is well known that all his visits to El Paso have coincided with scandalous smuggling, theft of cattle and other robberies, but since he does not operate in person, until now no one has been able to catch him in a resignation, or even discover the link that has established with the elements of his supposed gang.

"He comes here like any other dealer, he visits places of vice, gambles, he spends the money, he hangs out with the girls in the gambling dens and it seems that he does not do or have to do anything else in his life.

And yet these visits have a clear objective. It is like a general who, from a rear-guard position unknown to the enemy, leads a great battle and uses someone who, linking with him, moves the battalions and ends up winning the battles.

"We know quite a few things about him, enough to make him dizzy if we wanted to, but that doesn't lead to anything practical, because we had to have him locked up and his entire organization would be working methodically making it useless to raise the hunt.

"Tymson knows all the rangers in the Division, I mean all the ones there were up to now, and he is such a good physiognomist, that a face he has seen only once in uniform does not fade.

»This spoils any attempt at surveillance near him, because knowing them, he takes great care not to provide any clue that could lead us to the organization of his squad and to know who they are, how many and how they operate.

But now that some new elements have been admitted to our ranks, the captain has understood that a productive espionage can be attempted around Tymson, placing near him a Ranger who is completely unknown to him and of whom he cannot suspect anything. And by mutual agreement, we have decided to entrust this mission to him, which will be seconded by my brother in a double game in case it is necessary for him to intervene.

»In principle, it is a matter of visiting the gambling dens that he frequents until he is located and from that moment on, taking care to control all his steps, as well as the kind of people he deals with, because it is undoubted that among these people there must be the elements that are They come as liaison with the gang and those who transmit their orders underhandedly.

"Ultimately, you have to become Tymson's shadow without prejudice to Caro fulfilling other tasks such as monitoring and following in the footsteps of those who, by relating to him, may be suspected of belonging to his gang.

"We suspect that his presence in El Paso will coincide with some major operation to transfer arms or livestock to Mexico. On the other side of the divide, those who yearn to overthrow the emperor are working hard to achieve it, and their main need is weapons and livestock.

"From recent news we have received, we know that taking advantage of the noise of the demobilization, some deposits of weapons collected from the graduates have been stolen and those weapons, one day or another have to go to the Mexican revolutionaries if we do not prevent their departure.

And it must be prevented for several reasons. One, because they are weapons of the nation that may be necessary at any time; another, because they have a value that they scandalously steal from us, and another, because we are accused of blatantly favoring the civil struggle by affirming that the weapons used by the rebels are of our manufacture.

»The Government is harassing us so that at all costs we avoid these smuggling and plundering by discovering the smugglers and annihilating them, but it is not as easy as it is supposed to be from a desk.

«Now, we presume that we are presented with an opportunity to cover the mouth of the higher powers a bit by interfering with something valuable in that sense and if with this, we dismantle Tymson's gang and destroy all of them, that we will have won and fewer people against the one to keep fighting.

"You, being a stranger of that type, can be very useful. You are a man of war, you know many tricks of it, and with a little luck, since you have the rest, you may be able to do good service.

«I have ordered the purchase of a cowboy outfit with the measurements that his uniform showed that I am going to give him. At dawn you will leave the barracks unseen and from that moment on, you will apparently have nothing to do with the rangers.

"My brother will act separately, although you will find him somewhere that I frequent. We are not going to prejudge how you have to carry out your work, because it would tie up your initiatives. At your discretion we leave your action and the most effective way to communicate any news without you knowing about it.

"You will be one of the many dealers who roam El Paso, with nothing apparent to do. As long as their connection to the Division is not discovered.

»You, Caro, you also have your civilian clothes to move around without a uniform. I hope nobody recognizes you since you have been absent for three years and it will be very rare for someone to associate you with me.

"It would be very valuable to both of them if their performance were a success. You win promotions here, too, like in war, Harry, and you can wear your old badges again if you earn them the way I did by exposing a lot, but with success.

«I think that at the moment I have nothing more to say to you. Tymson is known here and the places he frequents the most are La Alegría de El Paso and El As de Corazones, both of which are located in the most central part of the city. I'll give you a description of the guy and with that and something he hears about in the gambling dens, you will end up locating him.

'I can't go show it to you because it would raise suspicions and you'd better believe that we have too much to worry about and have missed your presence.

Nothing matters to him if he is forced to move from here on some clue. At the inn where you stayed when you arrived here, there is a room requested for you and you will find your horse in the stables. If necessary, use it at will.

Harry, who had listened closely to the sergeant's statements, replied:

"I think it would be convenient for me to change my clothes right now and go directly to the inn. Here, it seems, I have nothing to do and the sooner I detach myself from this, the better.

"Sounds good to me. If you want, "he added, addressing Caro," you can go home for the night. You leave your uniform there and dress in civilian clothes.

"I will, Bob.

"And I don't tell them anything. Here is the opportunity to show whether or not they were born for Rangers. I will celebrate that the test is final for both of us.

"We will try, Sergeant.

Caro left the barracks to go to his cabin where he would spend the night and Harry changed his uniform for the clothes that the sergeant had prepared for him and prepared to start his performance.

Bob, who guessed in him a tough and determined man, gave him a friendly blow on the back and commented:

"Harry, my greatest pleasure will be to spend time with you seeing you wear those badges that you have had to give up when you change your Corps. Earn them and you will give me satisfaction, because I am not envious. If I went freehand, why wouldn't I like others to go up?

"Thank you, sergeant. I will do what is in my power and, if I do not ascend, at least they are happy with my performance.

And he left the barracks to go to the inn.

Bob had taken care in his absence to hire the lodging and to leave the horse in the stable, so he had no difficulty in settling in.

Once in his room, he sat on the edge of the bed and reflected on the best way to carry out the mission entrusted to him.

He had to watch Tymson's footsteps and keep an eye on him. Could this be easy in the case of a wise man who knew what was at stake with his exposed business and who would live with a hundred eyes open so as not to be surprised?

He didn't see it as very viable, but the order was short and he had to try whatever it was.

But suddenly, he had an idea. What if he searched and found a way to establish a relationship with Tymson and become part of his band? For those highly exposed businesses, quite a few men were needed, especially when it came to throwing caches into the river, because the rangers were very vigilant about the Grande and many times they had to deal with them and cross the cache by force of fighting, exposing and even losing men. . It wouldn't be easy, but if she was lucky enough to get involved with Tymson, she might.

And he decided not to leave until the next day what he could do that night. He would walk around the gambling dens and make arrangements to locate the person of the smuggler.

The signs the sergeant had given him were an orientation. Tymson was a man of about forty, tall, of medium flesh, dark, with a very neat little mustache, curly hair, and because of him and his skin he seemed to show Mexican blood. As the best identification detail, he should look at the lobe of his left ear that had a bite.

He believed that with these details he would not need to ask questions or be hesitant. That scar was the smuggler's best identification. And he took to the street ready to tour the gambling dens.

In La Alegría de El Paso he did not discover anyone who had any resemblance to Tymson and leaving this place he headed to El Ace de Corazones.

It was a better place, the animation was great and the noise was thunderous.

And since she didn't discover her man either, she decided to waste some time in case he appeared.

An embryonic plan had been forged and he would try to follow him as far as circumstances allowed, so he sat down at an empty table near a place where four undesirable-looking guys were playing poker and ordered a modest glass of brandy.

The waiter glanced at him. Such miserable customers did not seem to be very attached to the place, but he had to resign himself and serve it.

Harry made no intention of drinking it. He placed it on the tabletop and set about keeping an eye on the front door, following with keen interest everyone who made their appearance in the room.

It had been more than an hour and he was beginning to suspect that he was missing a good sleep, when he swung the door back and forth and a guy appeared who at first glance seemed to fit the description they had given him of the smuggler.

She stiffened by fixing her attention on him. As long as she couldn't see his ear, she couldn't be sure that he was the man she was interested in.

But meanwhile she examined him curiously. If he wasn't Mexican, he looked a lot like it and much more, because at that time he was dressed like a typical Sonoran native.

Good guy, handsome, carefree when walking, with the gesture of a man who knows himself to be tough and confident, he walked upright and challenging. His well-formed skeleton enhanced the clothes of good cloth and better cut, and it was not surprising that he attracted attention wherever he passed.

She was wearing a very shiny black velvet outfit. The trousers flared by the legs, the short and tight bolero, the white billionaire shirt, the scarlet sash, the narrow high-heeled shoes and on the head the classic very high and pointed hat with the huge wings slightly turned up. .

It must have been well known. Several greeted him as he passed and one shouted:

Hello, Tymson, what is your life?

"Hello, manito" he replied cheerfully "; I was just in Santa Fe to solve some business and I came to take a walk here so as not to forget this. I see that El Paso is very lively.

"As always, Tymson, especially for those who bring Mexican ounces to spend.

"Those are never lacking, compadrito, over there business is just good. This is what seems to be not going very well from what they tell me.

"The war has screwed up everything, but people are starting to want to work. After a year, things will return to their normal course.

"Then, after a year it will be a matter of coming back here, don't you think?

"And now that?

"Since I'm here, I'll have fun for a few days and then I'll go back to New Mexico, although maybe I'll go south to see how the ranches are there. I have an offer of large batches of antlers to sell and they may be interested here.

He separated himself from the one who had stopped him asking those questions and advanced towards the back. Someone was calling him from a table near Harry's and Harry was glad, because that way he would see him closer, since he would have to pass between his table and the one next to it.

The one who called him had a kind of rancher. He later learned that he was, and that he had sometimes traded with Tymson by selling antlers to him.

Tymson walked over to the table the rancher was occupying and as Harry had calculated, the straightest path was to pass between his table and the one next to it. With all his senses alert he waited for the supposed Mexican to cross the narrow passage and when he did, he moved the table a little. Tymson tripped over the rim and the brandy glass lost its balance and tipped over, spilling the liquid.

But Harry did not put aggressive theater in the protest, but, in a plaintive tone, exclaimed:

"You screwed me up, friend. What do I drink now if I only have twenty cents to pay for what I spilled?

Tymson turned and with a smile exclaimed:

"I'm sorry, cowboy, but don't be in a hurry, you won't run out of drinking. Here, to bring me health "and threw an ounce of gold on the table.

Harry pretended to look at her greedily and cried out:

"An ounce! I had forgotten the color of gold. Blessed are you that you can afford to give them generously when some of us would sell our souls to the devil to conquer a handful of them,

Tymson halted his advance and, looking at Harry, exclaimed:

Are you a cowboy?

"It was, now I don't know what the hell I am anymore. I fought three years in the army; chew you foolishly lead and then, when you no longer need one, there it is; compose them as you can, that you no longer serve me.

He said it with an accent of concentrated rage and Tymson, making the intention to withdraw, commented:

"Don't despair, cowboy, maybe the job you need will come along to earn what you want. Drink and don't be pessimistic "and continued on until he joined the one who had greeted him.

Harry thought he caught in those sentences a vague warning of something that might be proposed to him and decided not to move from the table. He called the waiter and showing him the ounce, ordered:

"A whiskey of the best! I want to toast to the health of that rumbous Mexican.

The waiter obeyed the order and shortly after, he presented the whiskey that Harry was savoring with delight.

Intimately he felt exhilarated. It had come to Tymson's attention that it was already something, but this could have its pros and cons. If he was not interested in her person, what she would have done was reveal herself to him and it would be very difficult for him to be able to stick to his body like a shadow to spy on his movements.

If, on the contrary, he could be interested, then ... at some point he would be searched instead of having to search for him.

And if he was this lucky, he would have successfully started to carry out his boss's instructions. He liked danger for the pleasure of avoiding it and savoring it, although afterwards the end was something uncertain that he could or could not overcome, depending on the case.

Tymson talked to the rancher for a while, and then he shook his hands goodbye and made up his mind to go into the game room. As he got up to go to the living room, he glanced at Harry, who raised his glass to give him the drink and the smuggler greeted him with an expressive wave of the hand.

Harry decided to wait. He might foolishly waste a few hours of the night, but an on-duty Ranger had no time of his own. Whatever his work demanded, he had to give it to him, even if for it he had to stand days and nights until he fell exhausted from the effort.

Chapter IV

BETWEEN PILLOS WALKS THE GAME

He had been sitting alone for more than an hour with the glass half consumed, when a figure appeared before him that he could not pinpoint where it had come from. It was about a guy in his mid-thirties, tall, well built, very dark and wearing an outfit similar to his. The apparition approached the table and saluted, saying:

"Are you bored, cowboy?

"A bit.

"Do you want to be distracted by playing dice?

"Thanks, but I am short of money.

"Devil, I see gold on the table!

"This ounce has just been given to me and it has to last until the devil takes me with him or finds a job. I can't play a penny on her.

Without knowing why, Harry guessed that the presence of the stranger was not something accidental and spontaneous, but a preconceived encounter and wondered if his plan had come to fruition and that this guy had some mysterious connection with Tymson.

His interlocutor seemed not to be convinced and running a seat he sat next to him, saying:

"That's another story, cowboy. Things are really bad around here and you can't find a job easily. The issue of livestock has been shattered.

"Livestock and apparently everything. I had illusions when they gave me the license believing that now it would take many pawns and I have found that there are all of us left over. The panorama is beautiful and pleasant.

"Indeed, it is not so easy to resolve the ballot.

"But you have to solve it. I have come to El Paso ready to solve the matter. If I don't find something soon, I will cross the river and march to the other side of the divide. I have been told that the Juárez supporters need brave men and they pay them well. If the devil is going to take you, let him take you in a buggy.

"Would you do that, cowboy?

"Why not? When a man looks for work and cannot find it, when he needs to eat and sleep and has no money for it, he has to look for it somewhere and in some way. You can't live off the air and if the government is not in a position to assure the lives of those of us who have exposed it through it, let it go to hell.

The intruder, after letting Harry vent, exclaimed;

"Do you know your trade well?

"Hey, I'm as cowboy as the most and I show that on the ground.

"Out of courage, how are you doing?

"The certificate is on my body with three scars from as many shots received.

"That being the case, it may not be difficult for you to find a job.

"Where and how?

"Here in El Paso.

"Tell me who can provide it, that I am looking for you. When I run out of this ounce I will have to get money from where it exists.

"For you somewhere?

"Yes. I have paid the inn for three days in the Plaza Vieja.

"Well, wait there for a message from me, I will find you and provide you with work.

"When?

"It didn't take long.

"That is very elastic. I can spend three days with this and the dinner paid; but no, and if I lose them, what do I do next?

"You will not lose anything because you will get paid from tomorrow, even if it takes a few days to start working.

"Who guarantees it to me?

"Me.

"And who the hell are you? I don't know him and it may be a joke. No, buddy, I can't play with time.

The stranger took another ounce from his pocket and put it on the table, saying:

"Do you think this guarantees a three-day wait?

"This is already speaking in gold. I can wait those three days.

"So do not talk anymore. In due time I will go in search of him.

"Can't I know more? To work you have to know what you are going to earn at least.

"Much more than they would give him in another team.

"Well, I see him very enigmatic.

"When it comes time to join the team I will give you more details. You have an ounce of advance and the promise of a better salary, is it little?

"Well, forgive me for being suspicious, but my situation is dark. I had my projects if I couldn't find work and I will put them off.

"You will lose nothing. Until I go looking for it.

He said goodbye to him and disappeared from the joint.

Harry didn't dare move in case everything spoiled, but common sense told him that this guy was an item in Tymson's service. He must have told her to approach him and that is why she had addressed him directly.

And if so, he guessed that he was about to go into the wolf's mouth. Now the important thing was to be able to communicate the news to Bob or the captain, but he had to move with lead feet. Perhaps in those three days that were taken to dispose of his services he was very vigilant and could not spoil what chance had made him win.

He retired to the inn and there he pondered how he would warn Bob. He could not go to the barracks or contact a ranger just in case, and as for writing, it was known that he had sent a letter to the Division.

And after much thought, he thought he found the solution. He would write a letter to Cynthia so that she could later deliver it to her brother. Writing to a woman was not at all striking, unless many things were investigated until the relationship that the girl had with the sergeant was ascertained.

Having written the letter, he put it away and the next morning he asked the stable boy:

How could I get a letter into the hands of a girl? I like the girl, you know, but I am not very easy at words to say what I want and ... with the pen it is looser. Then, after she knows my feelings well ... things are easier.

"I understand, cowboy, is the girl from here?

"He has a cabin half a mile to the east.

"To see the letter?

When he read the name, he replied:

"I guess what it is. I live with my mother at that address and when she leaves duty this afternoon I can deliver her.

"Thank you very much friend. Here, for the trouble "and handed him a dollar.

He had to trust the goodwill of the waiter for the letter to reach its destination.

The letter arrived and Cynthia, surprised, tore the envelope. Inside it was a four-sided sheet and a note. The note read:

> "Ms. Cynthia: Sorry to bother you, but the matter is very delicate and I must. I don't know of any other procedure for getting this important letter into the hands of your brother Bob, and I entrust it to you. It is extremely important that no one knows that I associate with the rangers. Please get it to Bob as soon as possible.
>
> Very grateful, Harry.

The young woman, intrigued, read the sheet and shuddered. From the contents he guessed that the ex-sergeant had been commissioned for a mission that was not only difficult, but very dangerous, since it involved nothing less than sneaking into a smuggling gang and Harry, apparently, had succeeded.

Wasting no time, he addressed his mother, saying:

"Mom, I'm going to the village.

"To what, my daughter?

"I have a letter from Harry, Caro's partner, to deliver to Bob.

"And why does he send you and not him?

"For many reasons, Mom, it is a matter of service. I'll explain it to you.

And without wasting time he headed to El Paso in search of his brother.

Bob was at the barracks. When he announced the presence of his sister, he felt nervous.

"What are you coming for? He asked, coming out to meet her.

"Bring you this. It's from Harry and he sent it to me.

The sergeant took the letter, intrigued, and as soon as he began to read it, his eyes shone fiercely.

"Okay, Cynthia, you can come back... Ah, if any more come bring them without wasting a minute.

"Bob, what is that man going to try?

"A very logical and very ambitious thing, Cynthia. Reclaim your sergeant stripes here in the rangers. Go and do not get into things you do not know.

And he dismissed her with his own brusqueness.

"He immediately reported to the captain's office.

"What is it, Bob? Walter asked.

"I think I have good news, my captain.

"Regarding what.

"To Tymson and his gang.

"Devil! As soon?

"You are right. His recommended has not wasted time and I cannot explain how he has managed to do something that can be very useful. See this letter you sent to my sister to give to me. You have been careful not to send it here in anticipation. Read, what counts in it is very tasty.

Indeed, Harry was briefly recounting his incident with Tymson and then his interview with the stranger. In his opinion, he must have been sent by the smuggler to hire him encouraged by what he had heard him say about his future job. He believed him desperately determined to do whatever it took to earn money and he had surely taken those three days to watch over him and be sure that he was completely isolated and had no communication with anyone.

At the end of the letter, he added:

"Do not write to me, or visit me, or do anything to get closer to me, but see how to watch my steps and those of the man who will come in search of me. I am determined to go where they want to take me and take part in what they try to serve as bait. As I will not be able to do more, it is up to you to follow my trail and the rest will be what fate has arranged.

Walter, after reading the letter, exclaimed:

"I think like Harry that there is a connection between Tymson and the guy who approached him by offering him a job.

"If so, that man has not wasted time and has achieved something that can be very useful. Seems to me like he's a gutsy guy and ready to go.

"That seems to me, the question now is to see how the trap is organized to get everyone who revolves around that issue into it. I understand what Harry is saying; It would be very risky for him to try to communicate with us and we are the ones who have to take care not to lose the bait. If that man does not regret it and ends up taking him away, it will be to put him in the gang and if we lose sight of them, he will find himself isolated and at the mercy of many dangers and a false situation that will be very difficult for him to overcome. It is necessary to study very carefully how things are going to be done, so that that little thread or those that may later derive from it do not break.

"That's right, my captain, and the bad thing is that we are not the ones who can follow the track because they would know us right away. This espionage mission must be entrusted to new and hitherto unknown men in the Corps, and of the few there are, I have no reason to place much trust in their sagacity and discretion. I have my brother who I will teach well and who I hope will not disappoint me, but of the other three or four new ones I do not know what capacity they will have for these things. It is not enough to be brave and reckless, even if they are, because those virtues are to be manifested at the last minute. At the moment, as things are presented, you have to have a man dedicated to following in Tymson's footsteps and another to follow the one who has hired Harry, once he is identified. Later, I don't know if it will take more to follow other leads.

"We will have to make do with what we have. Entrust one of those to follow Tymson and put his brother on the lookout for the inn for when they go to find Harry. Then, based on what they find out, we'll proceed.

"We will do our best, my captain. This case is not the vulgar case of chasing a gang of cattle rustlers or smugglers, because the gang is unknown. If it were only about meeting them, I have plenty of men of heart to do so.

"I take charge, but somehow you have to track them down. I leave it in your hands and I trust that everything will go well. What I will regret is that this man finds himself stuck in a bottomless pit from which it is not easy for him to get out. If, as he says, he is willing to go to the end, I fear that if we locate the gang and cut them off, the prize for him may be a bullet from his own companions.

"I do not know, a man of his qualities always finds resources to avoid danger, but if he is not, in the honor roll of the Division there are some names of heroes gloriously fallen in acts of service. His name would be one more in the box.

"I prefer him alive, Bob. The ones that are worth the most are the ones that we should lose the least.

"But without his sacrifice I don't know.

"They could have performed more valuable services. Whoever wears this uniform knows what they are exposed to and if they accept it, it is because they were born to ranger.

Bob parted from the captain in great concern. The matter was extremely delicate and he was going to bear a great deal of responsibility for its success or failure.

And what infuriated him the most was not being able to act in person. He did not trust anyone as he trusted himself and would have given up the badges to earn them again as long as he had had the freedom of movement to be able to support Harry.

But he would have to settle for entrusting this mission to his brother. He tasted brave and determined, but he was very suspicious of his poise. He was too young and impulsive, and he feared that he lacked the coolness necessary not to commit impetuosities that could ruin everything he had earned.

He had to go to his cabin to look for him since it had been agreed that he did not appear at the barracks. Caro had already heard from Cynthia of Harry's activities and was eager to get into action.

Bob was giving him a serious review to instill in him that he should proceed with measure and not get carried away with foolish impulses or conceited acts that could be harmful to everyone. He had to bear in mind that the enemy was going to have a very valuable hostage in his hands and that the life of this hostage had to be taken care of to the limit.

And after these recommendations, he entrusted him with the mission of monitoring Harry until he saw him contact someone. Then, he would abandon his partner to become the shadow of the other.

To keep an eye on Tymson, he chose from among the three new enlisted elements the one who seemed the most savvy and after giving him countless instructions, he ordered him to locate the smuggler and monitor his movements and, above all, take note of the people with whom he related.

Harry waited after that strange conversation with the stranger. True to his promise, he just waited and his life couldn't be more monotonous. He would get up late, walk through the city, make nightly visits to the joint, limiting himself to having a single most modest drink, and he had not exchanged conversation or a word with anyone.

If this was what they wanted to verify, they had to be satisfied with their behavior, for there could be no greater sense of isolation than theirs.

Several times he had discovered Caro guarding the inn or following him at a distance, but not a grimace, not a sneaky greeting, or anything that could be caught by eyes unfamiliar to him. Caro did not exist, although she knew he had become her shadow.

On the third night, after his visit to the gambling den, he returned to the lodge and when he reached it and opened the door to his bedroom, he found the individual with whom he had dealt with three nights before sitting on the bed. Harry looked at him in amazement and asked:

What the hell are you doing here?

"You see, waiting for you.

"And how did you get in?

"I have asked for accommodation and they have given me the adjoining room. As the keys are apparently single-lock, it has not been difficult for me to open and wait quietly for him.

"Very good and...

He stared at his little suitcase. It showed signs of having been opened and for a moment it was tense, but it was quickly redone. In anticipation of all the contingencies in her there was absolutely nothing that could compromise him.

What were you going to say?

"That if the possible employment contract also includes the freedom to search my luggage.

"It is possible, friend Harry.

He looked at him feigning distrust.

"Hey, I don't remember telling you my name or your saying yours.

"That doesn't matter. I knew his; mine will know in time.

"This seems too much of a mystery to me.

"I will convince you that there is no such mystery. I need a few men skilled in their trade, temperate, eager to earn money in the quickest way, but with guarantees that their people have nothing to do with elements that do not interest us at all. This is where the registration of your luggage comes in.

"What did I expect to find in him, a dragon with a hundred heads perhaps?

"Something similar, but now that I know he doesn't have him locked up, things vary.

»The work that we are going to do is very lucrative, we pay very well those who take part in it, but since it is something that certain elements do not like and they are after sticking their nose in them, we have to take severe precautions.

"Hmm! Contraband perhaps?

"Why do you suppose it that way?

"If we weren't in El Paso, if nothing more than the river separated us from Mexico and if I didn't know that arms and cattle pay well there, I wouldn't think so.

"Indeed, that is what it is all about. The stash is important, we need more people than we have and it has been necessary to look for a long time for some more men to help us and on whom we obtain the maximum personal guarantees.

"On one occasion, we were about to add a Ranger to our ranks. The thing was very well contrived, but he despised us too much and it was his undoing. He had allowed himself the luxury of hiding his Ranger badge in his suitcase, and they had to bury him with it.

Harry had to make a tremendous effort to appear indifferent. He, too, kept his whisk plate, but had been careful to sew it under the lining of his vest so as not to be seen.

And sketching a strange smile, he asked:

"So ... what I was looking for was one of those plaques.

"That or something I didn't like before closing the deal. Now I can tell you some things that I wouldn't have told you before.

"You have been spied on these three days and you have not taken a step that has been unknown to us. As we have verified that you do not have relationships with anyone, that you are completely alone and do not hide anything that could be harmful to us, the test has been happy for you and now we can speak without reservation.

"The job I offered you is still standing. It is about passing to the other side of the river an important cache of weapons for the Mexican revolutionaries. As it is something that they pay well, the boss pays his men well, therefore, you will earn in less than two weeks more than if you were working a year on a ranch.

"Well, the offer is tempting, but what about the danger?

"The danger is relative. We have passed many caches and even large herds without running into the rangers. We also have them under surveillance and we take care to control their movements. This is a fight in the shadows in which we try to make fun of each other and sometimes we make fun of them and other times they have some luck and they find us.

"But even so, many times it is not of much use to them because we are well armed, well prepared and with enough people to keep us from getting caught. More than once we have engaged in battle with them and we have kept them at bay in one place, while on another he was crossing the cache.

"It is true that sometimes, some have fallen for both sides, but this is a gamble that is compensated with the remuneration.

»What is prepared is very important and must be well guarded and well defended. Initially, the chief has assigned a thousand dollars to each man who helps the cache cross the river and later, if it arrives intact, there will be a premium according to the utility that is taken from the shipment. Later, if things go well and it is convenient for him to continue with us, he will charge a hundred dollars a month and a percentage of the new caches that are passed or the bundles that come to us. If not, once on the other side of the divide, your commitment may expire and with that money you can go where you want, because we will dissolve to erase the trail and we will rejoin where and when it is convenient.

»You wanted to go over to the Mexicans to join their side and save your pothole. You would not be paid as much or less exposed than with us.

"Well, I see that you are well informed about my thoughts. I don't deny that that was my idea, but it made it contingent on finding or not finding work. Of course, now I don't see work in perspective and between going to Mexico or accepting what he proposes to me, the choice is not doubtful: I am more interested in this.

"In that case, I let him sleep for a few hours because at dawn I will call him to come with me.

"Far away?

"You will already know that.

"I say this in case I have to take the horse or leave it here.

"You need the horse as much as your revolver.

"In that case, I am ready to go.

"Well, since it's late, go to bed. I will call you.

The smuggler was about to leave. Harry stopped him, saying:

"May I now know what I am to call you?

"Yes; My name is Morley.

"Well, nothing more; until the early morning, Morley.

When Harry was alone, he sat down on the edge of the bed in his turn and gave himself up to deep thoughts. His plan had worked well and he knew he was fully involved in Tymson's gang, but with that he had barely advanced anything.

From that moment on, he would be imprisoned in the networks of those tough people who did not forgive the slightest trace of betrayal. Morley had cynically confessed that the ranger who pretended a move like his had been buried with his badge and this warned him of the danger that he could run once tied to the meshes of that dark web.

But he wondered if he had solved something by running this dramatic adventure. Apparently, everything was done by surprise and quickly. They had watched him for three days as he had feared, and although Caro had made an effort to follow in his footsteps, nothing had been discovered.

Now he didn't know a word of what was going on either, because Morley had been careful to approach him in his bedroom without anyone seeing him or guessing about his relationships with him.

And they were going to leave at dawn. If, as was logical at that time, Caro was not hovering around the inn, they would disappear from El Paso without leaving a trace and he would find himself completely disconnected from the Division.

What could you do alone and without help? How could they find the trail if they disappeared like smoke? There was no room for him to leave a message to let them know his fate, for Morley had been very careful not to find out.

For Harry it was a problem that he did not know how to solve. For a moment he was about to leave the inn in silence, run to the barracks and give an account of what was happening, but what could he anticipate? Morley would be arrested or not, but this would surely not get to where the captain wanted to go, which was to have the entire crew in his hand, to be able to establish the responsibility that Tymson was responsible for and what was even more important, to know where was the stash to be able to intervene.

He couldn't do that. He had to let himself be carried away by the current like shipwrecked people and let it carry him to the saving beach or crash him against the cliffs.

All he could think of was to write a letter giving an account of the situation and get it into Cynthia's hands like the one above, but this was not easy, because Morley could be on the prowl until the last moment.

Yet it was the only viable thing, and he had to do it. After much thought, he made a decision. He undressed, turned off the light, and went to bed.

But he did not fall asleep and thus allowed more than two hours to elapse. The night was clear and a moonlight shone through the window.

At more than three o'clock he got up in silence, looked for a piece of paper and an envelope, and silently, in the moonlight, wrote the letter with a piece of pencil. Then he sealed it in the envelope and wrote the address on it.

He hid the envelope under the headboard with a note that read:

"Because you have to leave unexpectedly, please send this letter to your destination."

And with it he left three dollars for the volunteer who wanted to fulfill the request.

If the letter got into Cynthia's hands, Bob would know everything that happened, and what he could or couldn't do afterwards was up to him.

He ended up falling asleep and was in the best of sleep when a hand shook him, saying:

Come on, Harry, it's time.

The former sergeant threw himself out of bed, dressed almost asleep, and in five minutes he was ready. Morley did not leave him for a moment and accompanied him to the stable in search of the horse.

And it was beginning to dawn when they both left El Paso heading northeast.

As Harry had suspected, no one was watching the inn at this hour. They could not suspect that, so suddenly, without any margin to suppose the ranger in contact with the smugglers, they would take him away at such hours already.

The first news came by chance. The waiter in charge of cleaning the ranger's room discovered the letter, the note and the three dollars and understood that he should honestly earn them by delivering the letter.

When Cynthia received it, she asked the waiter:

"Did they say something to you when they handed it to you?

"Nothing, the guest left at dawn with a colleague and left it under the headboard. He has left without leaving a sign.

Cynthia felt a shudder throughout her body. He knew from Caro the mission that both had and guessed that the former sergeant had been forced to leave without being able to give more details than those contained in the letter.

He hurriedly ran to the village in search of Bob. Caro had left very early and must be fulfilling her mission.

When the sergeant received the letter and read its contents, the curses must have been heard across the river. They had not counted on that undesirability skill and had chosen a time when no one could suspect that the incident would arise.

Enraged, he sought out the captain to give him an account of the missive. Harry briefly explained what had happened and testified to what was already assumed. That they had searched for him by order of Tymson and that they had led him to join the squad by dismantling all contact with his companions.

But it did leave some useful information. A large-scale arms smuggling was being organized, and one day or another they would try to make it cross the river on the way to Mexico.

For want of something better, extreme vigilance was imposed not only along the river, but also in the landscape in the desert areas and, above all, in the part of the New Mexico divide, where by Las Cruces or some other town to the north, they could cross the river and then descend to Mexico, leaving El Paso below.

Walter was very upset at the news. For Harry all the compliments, because the ex-sergeant was exceeding in the line of duty and was providing as many details as possible, but his effort in breaking the connection with him could not only be null, but create a state of danger from which it was very difficult for him to get out.

Furious, he ordered:

"Bob, you need to not lose sight of Tymson in any way. It is the only thread that we have so that we do not get lost in nothingness and we have to keep it as it is.

The sergeant, angrier than he, growled:

"I'm going to take care of you, my captain.

"It will be a waste of time, because even the red ants of the desert know you.

"I know, but I'm going to make sure they don't know me. I will disguise myself the best that I can and know how, and I will constitute myself in its shadow. If I manage to mislead him, fine, and if not, I will expose myself to whatever it takes. I don't even trust myself anymore.

"Well, organize it as you see fit, but be careful to follow in that vulture's footsteps. If, as it seems, it is his gang, when he has completed the supply of men he needs, he will disappear from here without a trace and we will no longer hear from him until the cache tries to cross the river, or has crossed it, laughing at us .

"We will see that, my captain.

Bob, stung by his self-esteem, got ready to carry out his plan, but not before highlighting two pairs of Rangers to try to locate any trace of the missing couple. They had gone out on horseback at dawn, and perhaps in the landscape they could locate a trace, although he did not trust it.

For his part, he bought a disused miner's outfit from a used clothing store. It consisted of very wide blue trousers that he tied to his knees with a rope, high-heeled boots worn with leggings almost to the knee, a gaudy plaid shirt and a yellow vest ditto, plus a hat with flabby brims and a worn crown. all of which made him look like a defeated miner.

Then, he smeared his face with black smoke, blackening his already weathered face and to further disguise his face, he painted his eyebrows enlarging them. In fact, only on close examination could he be recognized as Sergeant Bob Reggs of the El Paso Rangers.

Chapter V

A TRAGIC PERSECUTION

Harry had been missing without a trace for three days. The efforts of the Rangers to search for his tracks were useless and from that moment on, they did not hear a word from the brave ex-sergeant.

Bob, completely disguised, was keeping an eye on Tymson from a distance, who seemed unaware of the surveillance, as he continued to lead an ostentatious life in the gambling dens, without revealing more relationships than normal between people who were known in El Paso and in El Paso. the one that was not suspected of being involved in such dangerous matters as those.

Caro alternated with her brother in the task of spying on the smuggler. After Harry's failure, Tymson's steps were monitored day and night.

Bob was determined not to lose sight of him and to discover whoever was associated with him and to follow in their footsteps until he found his missing partner.

But the dealer did not appear to be in a hurry. He was leading his ordinary life and nothing denounced that he was about to disappear from El Paso.

In the evenings, after having dinner at the hotel, he would go to El Ace de Corazones where he alternated with one of the girls from the cast, or spent a couple of hours in the gaming room, before, around two, retiring to his accommodation. .

Bob, trying to hide as much as possible, waited patiently for him in a corner of the bar and when he came out, he slipped like a dense shadow sheltered in the facades of the houses and followed him until he was convinced that he was definitely retiring to rest.

The sharp sergeant was convinced that before long he would disappear from El Paso, and he was alert to all his senses. He expected an unforeseen maneuver from the smuggler and did not want to be surprised.

For this reason, when he left him at the hotel late at night, he was not convinced that he was actually retiring to rest and would remain in ambush for a long time in the surroundings, until Caro, who was in charge of watching over him while he slept, espionage charge.

The gambling den was located on Montana St., at the intersection with Piedras Copia and the mysterious subject was staying at the Texas hotel, installed on Wyoming St. that was parallel to the previous one.

Tymson ostentatiously left the joint, crossed from one street to another along one of the side alleys, and disappeared inside the hotel.

Bob, as always, took up positions at the corner of the alley under the shade of a warehouse shed and waited patiently. He would stay at his post for an hour as usual and then leave Caro until the next morning.

Half an hour later he felt cautious steps and looked suspiciously, but calmed down. It was Caro who came as usual.

"Nothing, Bob?

"Nothing, Caro, and yet a sixth sense tells me it's about to disappear. I would like to suffer from the insomnia disease to spend my life glued to the heels of his boots.

Caro made an observation:

"Do you think it can easily disappear at an exotic time? I know positively that you don't have a horse here and to leave El Paso, you will have to use the train.

"Don't trust that. No one has been able to link him to any suspicious subject and yet he arranged everything perfectly to take Harry away without anyone knowing. No one can assure you that at a certain moment they do not wait for you somewhere with a good horse and try to disappear.

"Yes, it is true, and I am thinking that if that were the case and we found that they were waiting for him with a horse, we could not do anything to follow him, because we would not have time to look for our mounts. Have you thought about that, Bob?

"Not; It has suddenly occurred to me now and I don't know how we are going to organize that if it arises. Tomorrow I will have a few of our men stand guard on horseback at strategic locations on the outskirts. Thus, if it happened, what just occurred to me, I would soon have a horse to follow in her footsteps.

More than an hour had passed and Bob, convinced that nothing would happen that night, prepared to leave his brother and go to the barracks, but when he was about to leave, he clung closer to the shadow and squeezed Caro's arm so that be still.

Someone had just appeared at the door of the hotel and although at that hour, the light was poor, yet Bob's sharp gaze recognized the smuggler.

"My heart did not deceive me," he murmured. Tymson is going to disappear from here like a shadow.

Tymson did not carry a briefcase or anything that denounced such a purpose. He appeared dressed as when he entered and it gave the impression of going out to take the cool of the night rather than to flee.

Tymson looked up and down until he was convinced that at that hour the road was deserted and at a normal pace, without haste or nervousness, he continued down to the west.

At the end of the street and to the left, was the Unión Estación, but at that hour no train was circulating. However, passing it and crossing Santa Fe St., you reached the river and in front of the international bridge.

Bob thought he guessed Tymson's idea. He would not go by train, but would use the various boats that made the journey along the river bank to get away and disembark somewhere far away where they would surely be waiting for him.

He had to check it and if so, follow him in the same way. It wouldn't be difficult at all to jump into one of the moored boats and dash downstream behind whatever boat the smuggler could use.

When he got far enough to be able to follow him at a distance without being seen, Bob lunged after him followed by his brother and skimming the facades of the buildings they followed at a distance.

Tymson, unconcerned about taking any precautions, followed the street to the end, twisted around the station that was silent and dark, and down Santa Fe St. he reached the river.

The two Rangers, like stalking wolves, followed as closely as possible. Tymson approached the shore, descended a little until he reached one of the ladders, and descended them. At the foot of the steps that plunged into the water there was a boat waiting for him.

The smuggler jumped at him and standing on the deck looked down humorously. Then he waved his hand goodbye and the boat rolled off the shore into the center of the stream.

In the dark enough night, the position lanterns of the boat were the only thing that could be distinguished, the rest was confused with the black mass of the water.

Bob ran to the shore, determined not to lose sight of such a dangerous element, and followed by his brother reached the edge of the river.

Near where Tymson had disappeared was a long boat with two men in it. Some nets that hung from the sides denounced them as fishermen. Bob beckoned to Caro and they both descended the ladder while Bob called the fishermen.

"Quick, friends, bring the boat closer here. We need it.

"Hey" said one ", we too. We have to fish and ...

"Quick, without wasting time. Ranger K Division special service. The damage caused to them will be paid.

The order was strict and the command of such a tough authority as the rangers could not be disobeyed. The two fishermen, without any objection, released the rope, loosening it so that the boat could slide up the ladder.

When they got to it, they grabbed the line and Bob jumped on deck, but one of the fishermen growled:

Hey, what joke is this? You said they were Rangers ...

"Don't waste a second or I'll throw you in the water," Bob bellowed. I'll show you later, but let go of that damn line for now and follow that boat that took off just now. Keep an eye on the stern lantern or I'll hold you responsible for something very dangerous.

Before the severe order, the two fishermen were forced to definitively release the line that fell into the water and, taking the oars, they pushed the boat in to carry out the order.

The red position lantern on the boat that Tymson was traveling into was dwindling dangerously, and Bob was afraid of losing it in the shadows of the night.

"Remen de firme," he ordered, "and when they reach enough for him not to escape them, put down the oars and let the current take us.

The order was obeyed, but one of the fishermen, not yet convinced, growled:

"You have promised to show us that you are Rangers. I think we have the right to be convinced.

Bob unbuttoned his shirt and in the light of the forward lantern showed him the square lit on the inside while saying:

"Are you convinced now? I'm Sergeant Bob from Division K. Haven't you heard of me?

"Oh yeah, Sergeant Bob! But in that suit ...

"That is the least. Go ahead, I absolutely need to keep track of that boat.

"What happens? Some gunman who escapes you?

"Something more than that; a smuggler that I need to take into custody.

The boat, propelled not only by the hard current, but by the two fishermen's oars, flew over the surface of the river in thick eddies to the right and left, but Bob was unaware of the splash of the water. Standing in the center of the boat, he looked eagerly for Tymson's boat that was now closer, for it was only being carried away by the current.

When he calculated that they had gained enough distance and that they would not lose sight of him, he ordered:

"Turn off those lights.

Hey, not that. We may stumble upon some other boat.

"I do not expect. I need them not to know that we are following them. At least take down the headlamp and leave it here on the bottom. That they do not see the light and do not suspect that we are going to reach them. If they realize it, things are not going to be very easy and what I want is not to hunt that man, but simply to follow him.

The command was reluctantly obeyed and the red forward lantern, once down, remained at the bottom of the boat, painting the feet and legs of its occupants in red.

The fishermen had left their oars inside the boat and were being carried away by the rushing current. At a distance of about sixty yards, the boat leading to Tymson was still gliding swiftly down the center of the stream.

Bob, hunted by the hunt, stood in the center of the boat with his gaze fixed on the fugitive boat, while his brother, sitting on one of the benches with his elbow on the gunwale, was also staring at the boat.

The two fishermen, apparently indifferent to what the two rangers were so worried about, had positioned themselves one aft and one forward. The one in the stern had Bob's back, while the other had Caro on his side.

And suddenly, when the two brothers were more distracted, following the march of the opposite boat, at a gesture from one of them, the one with his back to Bob wielded a heavy stick that rested on the bench and with savage momentum lifted it to leave it. fall on the head of the sergeant, while the other threw himself on Caro.

And it was lucky for Bob that a whirlpool of water made the boat rock and caught him off guard, forced him to tilt his body to one side, making him almost lose his balance.

This sideways movement prevented the thick stick from crushing his head, but it did not prevent it from landing on his left shoulder.

Quick reflexes, Bob realized that they had entered a death trap themselves. The boat was there like bait in anticipation of Tymson being followed, and the two fishermen were nothing but smugglers on duty.

And as Bob was hard as flint, despite the fierce pain produced by the blow, he stirred quickly and withstood the second jam of the smuggler, who when missing the blow as he had also suffered the imbalance of the boat, could not stay upright to apply Quickly a second blow and, realizing the reaction of the ranger, tried to grab him in any way with the intention of throwing him into the water.

Bob gripped him fiercely and both fought in that narrow and dangerous field of fight in a deadly duel, while Caro, caught by surprise, sitting next to the gunwale, struggled to get rid of the pressure of his enemy who was trying to squeeze his neck with eagerness murderers.

The boy, in a supreme effort to free himself from death, managed to drive his knees into his chest, pulling him back. The false fisherman could not keep the pressure on the boy's neck and was forced to release his hands to, immediately, receive a terrible kick in the chest that sent him backwards.

But the width of the boat that danced in the harsh ungoverned current was so precarious that the bandit when he fell, struck his spine on the opposite rail, tipped over and slid into the water.

The boat twisted dangerously, Bob and his fiercely locked enemy lost their balance, they also fell on that side and the boat overturned violently, throwing the four into the water.

Caro jumped like a ball from the other side drawing a parable in the void to follow the castaways.

In a quick view of the drama, Caro saw her brother struggling in the waves without letting go or being released by his enemy and how the two disappeared for a moment under the water. Then he confusedly saw his rival swimming hard toward him and saw a long, heavy oar skim past him.

Instinctively he grabbed it to help himself stay in the water, just as his rival, swimming vigorously, came up to him. Caro, a good swimmer, stroked with one arm and raised the oar, letting it fall on the smuggler's skull. This one disappeared under the water and no longer saw more.

The current was driving him away impetuously and despite the anguish that thought about his brother's fate caused him, his instinct for self-preservation moved him to take care of him and, allowing himself to be carried away by the current, he swam cautiously.

No trace of the boat and its occupants. God knew what had happened to them, but he hoped that his brother had been the same luck and was swimming in the river.

He raised his head and looked ahead. The lights of the boat where Tymson was traveling were revealed at a safe distance and his ranger instinct told him that, despite everything, he had a mission to fulfill and he must fulfill it.

If it was possible for him to stay afloat, he would follow the boat to where it landed and if not, his luck would be bad, but he would not remain for lack of courage.

Cautiously, she began to cut the current at an angle to swim closer to shore. In case of exhaustion it would always be easier for him to land than having to overcome the center of the flood.

And raising his head from time to time, he looked eagerly for the hunted boat, fearing that he would lose sight of it.

Until one of the times he observed that the boat was also looking for shore little by little and this told him that it was trying to land.

And so it was. Upon reaching a place where the river formed a backwater, the boat turned in danger of capsizing and headed for the gap where the backwater was produced. For a moment it seemed that the momentum of the water was going to prevent him throwing him against the shore.

But he was skilfully saved and the little boat entered the already quiet backwater.

Caro, afraid of being thrown into it by discovering those people, swam vigorously looking for the shore before reaching the place where the boat had penetrated and when brushing against some lustful growing bushes protruding above the riverbed, he stretched out his arm and managed to cling fiercely at them. The bush resisted the pull and Caro managed to get close to the ground until she jumped into it.

He was broken, exhausted, gushing water like a small spring, but his indomitable spirit remained intact and rising to his feet, he decided to advance towards the pool.

He came forward in pain, trying to orient himself. The starlight made it difficult to achieve, but it favored him not to be discovered.

Until suddenly he heard the sound of voices and, advancing more cautiously, approached the place where they were speaking. There were several people who had gathered.

And now close to the group and close to the ground, he was able to catch a voice, Tymson's, saying:

"You will continue with the boat to San Elizario and hide it there. The rest you already know. We will head to Ciudad de Juárez and in just a week in La Mesa. Do not waste time in case someone has tried to follow us, which I seemed to observe, although the lights we saw when we left soon disappeared. Anyway, you have to give the rangers the value they have and don't forget that they also give me a value.

Caro, hearing the smuggler's instructions, was left suspended for a moment. In the embarrassment of the shipwreck, he had not realized that they had gained shore on Mexican soil and for this reason, Tymson spoke of going to Ciudad de Juárez and later to La Mesa. It would be very easy for him to enter New Mexico across the border nation divide and pass El Paso leaving him behind.

A sound of horses moving inland told him that the smuggler and those who were waiting for him were moving away, while the boat was half stranded in the mud of the backwater.

And the brave boy wondered what he could do. He was on the land of Mexico and to get back to El Paso he had to cross the Grande again and walk a distance that he calculated by the time they had been on the river of about twelve or fourteen miles. And the feat seemed to him superior to what his exhausted forces could yield.

Chapter VI

A HEROIC FEAT

Shivering from the cold from the long stay in the water and the constant dampness of her clothes, Caro didn't know what decision to make. To jump into the river at night to cross it in that gloom and with his strength broken, it was crazy. The least he could do was wait for the day to clear and his energies to recover a little.

He had found out something; This could be very useful, since they had a period of one week to get to La Mesa and in that time they could return to El Paso to give an account of their odyssey and organize what was necessary to take over the gang or locate Tymson, but there were other more immediate things that filled his attention.

One was the anguish of not knowing the fate of his brother. Bob was tough, energetic, brave to the point of recklessness, but the river had swallowed tough men like himself and he couldn't rule out that misfortune had struck him down.

Just by pondering it the pain lacerated his chest. What would happen at home when his mother and sister heard of Bob's bad luck?

It is true that he had been about to suffer the same bad luck, but he had been saved and the penalty of being great would not be paroxysmal.

Then he would think of the ridicule they had been made the object of. His brother, despite his knowledge and cunning, had locked himself in that death trap and his enemies would be laughing at them greatly, although it was possible that some of those who manned the false fishing boat, in particular the one who hit him with rowing, they were doing it at the bottom of the river.

But apparently the gang was long and made up of men of steel. His two fierce enemies had proved it, and there he had next to him two others who could not be disdained.

And suddenly he conceived a crazy project. He needed the boat to cross the river more comfortably and if there was a way to get hold of that couple of undesirables, perhaps their reports would be very valuable, apart from the fact that, if he managed to carry out the feat, it was very easy that he would be worth some reward that he would have well won.

The two crew members of the boat did not seem to be in a hurry to leave the backwater to continue on the river to their destination. The night was very bad to maneuver across the barrier and the eddy of the river to beat and form the backwater and prudence seemed to advise them to wait for the light of day.

This was going to be very dangerous for him if he didn't get away from there, because they could discover him and the disproportion of forces to fight would be enormous. He tired and unarmed and those two guys carrying revolver on their waist in complete safety.

But he was haunted by the idea of getting hold of them. It would be a spectacular and brave blow that would credit him in the eyes of his teammates and in particular his captain. He was still without firing, he had not received the baptism of blood from the Rangers and he had to make it clear that his brother had not trusted him in vain.

The two boatmen had remained close to the shore without deciding their attitude. They seemed to meditate a lot and both were silent.

Until one asked:

"What do we do, James?

"I do not know. I do not like to go out to the river in this darkness. You know how dangerous it is to collide with the flood and line the boat inside it. During the day there are more possibilities and if something happens, we could swim better on land.

"You're right, but what do we do here alone? There are at least three hours until dawn.

"What if we lay down to sleep for a while until sunrise? There is no soul here and we can do it safely.

"Well, you have given me an idea. We have plenty of time to take the boat with the others and return to the place of the appointment. Well, let's find a place to lie down. We have spent the night awake and three hours of rest will not be bad for us.

Caro, hearing them, flattened herself among the willows that grew at the edge of the pool. He couldn't be wetter than he was, and he couldn't get into the water a little more than a little less.

It would not be there where the smugglers sought their makeshift bed, as they would do so on dry ground away from the humidity.

From his hiding place he was able to follow the movements of one of them. He circled within the range of his gaze looking for the right place to improvise his mat.

At last she saw him bend down about twenty yards, pile leaves at the foot of a long bush, and spread a blanket, which he went to fetch from the boat. The bed improvised, he lay down on it ready to take advantage of those three hours.

He could not see the companion, but he felt him move not too far, until at last he had to find the desired place because he stopped making noise.

Then he called:

"James, as soon as the sun hits our faces, upstairs.

"Do not worry. With a light sleep I will be ready.

And they did not change a word again.

Caro slipped out of the willows and chose less muddy ground. The fever that caused him to think that he could take over that pair of undesirables made him forget the physical torments of his situation and he felt revived to carry out the feat. But he would have to wait a reasonable time for those two guys to be overcome by sleep. He needed it because he couldn't fight both of them at the same time.

Counting the minutes, seeming to him centuries how long it took to pass, he waited in a terrible state of nervousness. He was going to play a dangerous trick and if he failed him in the least, it would have been useless to save himself from drowning if he fell riddled with bullets.

At last, devoured by impatience to resolve this dire situation once and for all, he armed himself with a thick, pointed stone that he had found among the willows and began to crawl across the ground like a reptile arcing to approach the sleeper from behind. He was in less danger of being seen and would have the smuggler's head closer to hand to strike mercilessly.

Because his success lay in surprising him and nullifying him with a fierce blow that did not allow him to scream.

If he succeeded, he would strip him of the revolver and with a gun in his hand he was not afraid of the other if he did not manage to hunt him asleep too.

Holding his breath, advancing smoothly so as not to make any noise, he gained ground. Little by little he was closing the gap and there came a time when he found himself less than a yard from his enemy.

He stopped to catch his breath, then advanced a little more, got to his knees and, lifting the stone with a sure arm, he chose the place of the blow.

The stone dug into the side of the smuggler's forehead, opening a good gap through which blood leaped. The smuggler shuddered, shrinking tragically, and Caro's hand clutched his victim's neck in case she could still scream, but no pressure was necessary, because that gesture was the only one he could execute.

Caro gasped and searched the wounded man's waist. There was the revolver, a .45 Colt with a heavy iron butt, and he gripped it eagerly. Now, with him in hand, he believed himself invulnerable.

This time he did not crawl on the ground, but walked on his feet, silently, looking for the undesirable other. The revolver was a good brake if it had the misfortune to be discovered early.

At last he located it. As confident as his partner slept on his back. Caro tiptoed forward, now brandishing her revolver by the barrel. It seemed more effective for hitting without killing the butt of the revolver, fearing that the stone had caused more than a blackout for the other smuggler.

He dropped to his knees, raised his arm, and struck.

When the ruffian received the blow, he emitted an impressive howl and had the courage to try to get up, but a second blow to the base of the skull annulled him in a fulminating way.

Caro, smiling, stood up. He had had crazy luck to carry out his audacious plan and now he felt possessed by such great joy that by effect of his nerves he had removed all the symptoms of fatigue from him.

The most difficult was achieved. Now, he only had to find some rope in the boat, tie them up and gag them well and drag them to the boat.

Once in it, he would cover them with the blankets so as not to attract attention and he would take the boat out of the backwater. Going upstream with that load was absolutely impossible, but he hoped that due to river traffic some cargo barge or steam launch would come upstream. If so, invoking his ranger status, he would ask for a line to tie up the boat and tow him to El Paso.

When dawn broke and he approached the wounded, he was impressed. Both had deep wounds on the head from which blood was flowing and, not knowing how to stop the small hemorrhage, he chose to put pieces of grass in the cuts of the wounds. The compress was not very effective and healthy, but in part it succeeded.

Then he dragged them to shore and gathered up the blankets. In the boat he found ropes that served to tie them well and once these wise precautions were taken, he saw and wished to put them in the boat.

Several times he was on the point of knocking him over, but finally, sweating like a condemned man, he deposited them on the bottom and covered them with the blankets.

And as the sun was already beginning to shine, he put himself at the oars and threw himself out of the pool in a very dangerous maneuver that could overturn the boat and send the three into the water.

But he was not a rookie in these struggles. He had rowed a lot in that river and had swum a lot in it and with patience and skill, putting his nerves and intuition to work, he managed to overcome the shock of the water and enter the current.

She began to drag the boat downstream, and Caro tried to counter the momentum with the oars. It was a titanic task that he could not accomplish.

He looked back in anguish. A paunchy, squat barge was trudging up the river. Caro, with all the power she could put into her voice, yelled:

"Hey, from the barge! A corporal, drop a rope or the flood will carry me away!

A bearded boatman took notice and threw a thick rope that ended in a wide loop and shouted:

"Attention, I loose rope.

Caro gripped the bow with her left hand tightly and raised her right arm. The boatman skillfully threw the rope at him and Caro managed to grab it through the hole in the rope. The jerk he felt when the boat was stopped seemed to tear off his arm, but he held steady and the boat stopped sliding downstream.

He put the rope through the tiller, holding it so that it would not come off, and soon he saw himself astern of the barge pulled by it.

The skipper of the boat approached, asking:

"Where the hell were you intending to go with that boat upstream?

"To El Paso.

"Well, you would have arrived when the frog grew hairs. What are you wearing under those blankets? You won't tell me it's contraband.

"Almost, boss. Watch it to convince you.

And he lifted a pick from a blanket showing the head of one of the smugglers.

The boss, seeing her all bloody, bellowed:

"By the beard of the prophetal! What does that mean?

"Don't be alarmed, boss. Do you know this? He opened his wet shirt and showed him the badge. The boss was well acquainted with the insignia of the Corps.

"Ranger?

"That's right. I have been hunting for two dangerous elements and I have managed to hunt them away from El Paso; I had no other means of transportation than the boat and I need to get them there.

"Well ranger, that's something else. We will arrive in El Paso mid-day.

The skipper did not worry more about his towage. Rangers were too serious and people who didn't have to fear them admired and appreciated them.

Caro was possessed of extraordinary joy. The feat he had just accomplished would have been signed by his brother with pride and he was sure it would cause a sensation in the barracks.

But her joy was squashed into sadness when she invoked the figure of her brother. If he had died in the river, all this would be indifferent because for him and his family, Bob's life was above all.

But since he knew nothing specifically yet, he hoped that Bob had risen from danger like he had and if so, the journey would have been glorious for both of them.

As the skipper of the barge had predicted, the vessel arrived in El Paso at noon.

Caro was looking forward to arriving because, although her clothes had partly dried due to the action of the morning sun, they felt damp and sticky on her flesh, causing her a feeling of nervous discomfort, apart from the fact that her stomach demanded attention that she had not been able to. offer.

Added to this was the longing to know if his brother had been saved from the catastrophe and was back in the city. If so, Bob must also have been distressed at not having the slightest news from him.

And finally, he longed to get rid of that annoying load and see them well guarded in one of the barracks cells.

The barge arrived at the river embankment and moored. The boss, addressing Caro, indicated:

"We have arrived, Ranger; now what?

"Would you like to do the full favor?

"What is it about?

"That one of his unloaders looks to see if there is a fellow guard on the boardwalks and tells him to come. I need help.

"Wait, I'll order them to find their companions.

Twenty minutes later, a uniformed ranger was leaning over the edge of the boardwalk.

Who is asking for my help? "I ask.

Caro indicated with her hand:

"Get down and get on the boat. Here I will tell you.

The ranger descended the ladder and got into the boat. Caro introduced herself, saying:

"As I have just joined the Corps, we are not known. My name is Caro Reggs and I am Sergeant Bob's brother.

"So nice to meet you. I heard a brother of the sergeant was coming in, but I hadn't had the pleasure of seeing him.

"The thing is that as soon as I entered a service was ordered in which I had to dress in civilian clothes and not appear at the barracks so that they would not identify my personality. Here's my badge.

"Enough, tell me what you wanted.

"Do you know if my brother has returned to the barracks?

"I have not seen him. This morning I took the service, but I did not see him. It is true that I do not belong to your company.

"I was afraid of it. Something dramatic happened to us last night on the river and I'm afraid he drowned.

"Do not say that.

"Yes, the story is long, but I don't have time to tell it. I need to get this out of here and take it to the barracks.

He lifted the blankets a bit and showed the bodies of the two smugglers. The ranger winced at his impressive appearance.

"Rays of hell! Where did you find that?

"In the river. I had to knock them out because my revolver didn't work. They are arms smugglers.

"Good service, mate. What should I do?

"I think it would be best if you go back to the barracks, look for Captain Walter and tell him that Caro, Sergeant Bob's brother, is in a boat next to the seawall with two wounded and deprived smugglers that they need to be transferred there. He will arrange what he deems most convenient.

"Well; I'm going to let you know right now.

Half an hour later the captain appeared with four rangers who carried poles and tarps to improvise two stretchers. The captain descended into the boat and greeted Caro, asking:

"What are you bringing, boy?

"This.

The captain took one look at them and said;

"Well, we'll talk later. The first thing is to take these carrions. Where is your brother?

"That I would like to know. I fear that at the bottom of the Great.

"Hey? What are you saying?

"I dont know. It was a terrible thing, Captain, and I'm afraid ...

"Well, don't talk now. We're going to evict this.

The rangers quickly assembled the stretchers, the bodies of the prisoners were removed and deposited on them and shortly after, they headed to the barracks.

The curious had tried to mill around at the foot of the boardwalk to browse the operation of the Rangers, but the one who had brought the warning took great care to keep them at a distance so that they would not hinder the maneuver and, above all, so that they would find out as little as possible about it. things that could be detrimental to release into public comment.

Chapter VII

A MAN OF NERVE

When they arrived at the barracks, the captain ushered Caro into his office and questioned him:

"Come on, boy, tell me everything that happened.

Caro, her voice cut short by the pain of not hearing from her brother, gave a detailed account of their odyssey that night on the river. It was a dramatic story that the captain appreciated with all its nuances.

And he was pleased with the grain, the nerve, the daring and the courage of the new Ranger at his service. He had not denied the family tradition and had received a baptism of blood on his body that would deserve a very prominent mention in the daily report.

"Bravo, boy! "He commented enthusiastically", you have behaved wonderfully and I am proud that you belong to my company. The feat has been worthy of a ranger and that credits you as one of the best.

"You have done something very useful, not only to track down the smugglers, but to be able to locate the whereabouts of your partner Harry, who we cannot abandon to these rogues. Tymson has been very clever, I admit that and he has shown that he does not trust anything to chance.

»He knows that he is being spied on and was prepared to evade any persecution. Anyway, this time his cunning has been broken and he has left something in our hands.

Now we know that something is being prepared in La Mesa for a week from now and unless the lack of these guys puts them on their guard and their plans change, something can be done.

"When the doctor treats those toads and they come to themselves, we will see what they have inside to release, but in the meantime I feel as uneasy as you about the fate of your brother and I am going to give immediate order so that a record is verified throughout the river and request information to the riverside towns in case they could have reached one, or if they had discovered a corpse in the river. It would be a painful loss for all of us if Bob had drowned. I know he was an excellent swimmer, but it all depended on his fight with the smuggler and how he was physically to save the momentum of the river.

"We must not lose hope, boy, because as long as there is no certainty of his death, it is possible to know about him.

"My God, what do I say now at home? For my mother it will be a terrible blow.

"I think the wise thing to do is not go there yet. As long as we do not have a certainty of her disappearance, it is not necessary to alarm her and give her annoyance if nothing has happened later. The bad news the later the better.

"As for you, you must be surrendered and broken, and a rest is convenient for you. Go to the mat and try to sleep a few hours; we'll take care of the rest.

Overcome by emotion, nerves, and exhaustion, Caro retired to the dormitory sheds, and soon the entire barracks learned with the consequent anguish the disappearance of Sergeant Bob.

Captain Walter ordered the mobilization of all available men, both the francs on duty and those who did not have an unavoidable mission, and pairs of horsemen at full gallop disappeared down the river bank to investigate the whereabouts of Sergeant Reggs.

His odyssey had been as dramatic as his brother's, though in another sense.

Bob fell into the water in a fierce embrace with the smuggler who had hit him. Despite the pain in his shoulder from the blow he received, his rough nature prevailed and he threw himself into the fight ready to dominate his enemy who was not soft either. The two like two rabid cats had fiercely gripped each other trying to get hold of each other's neck to decide the fight.

And in this hard embrace they were surprised by the fall into the water. Bob, who at that moment had the worst part because his left arm did not respond with the necessary strength and rigidity, felt the pressure of his enemy's hands, as he tried to free it with his knees to the stomach and thus, when he fell, he saw canceled to face the new danger.

The flood rolled them like a ball, making them roll at the stroke and submerge. Conservation instinct forced the smuggler to release his prey to swim and afloat.

Bob, being released from the pressure, was on the verge of not being able to float again. He felt a great suffocation and in a mechanical action he tried to breathe to bring air into his lungs and it was the water that entered his mouth, on the point of suffocating him.

In a brutal reaction he flailed his legs to rise to the surface and succeeded. Now free, his head sucked in eagerness and he tried to swim for shore. His shoulder ached horribly and he feared that he would not be able to stay afloat for long without the proper help from his sore arm.

And when, letting himself be carried away by the current, he swam with one arm to rest the other, something jumped on him; it was the body of his enemy that, when it also emerged from under the water, was swept away by the flood.

The smuggler was swimming more vigorously, perhaps because he was not stunted, and Bob felt the sensation that he was trying to get on top of him to see if he could finally sink him.

Instinctively, Bob dived to let him pass overhead and came out again several yards later, tripping over the body of his enemy as he surfaced.

And instinctively he reached out as he swam with the aching man. As he extended it, he tripped over the smuggler's boot and gripped it tightly. His enemy, feeling seized and lacking the movement of that oar so precise for his salvation tried to stir, but Bob, with the granite hardness of his nature and character, took a deep breath, took air into his lungs and submerged himself as far as he could dragging. behind him the body of his enemy seized by the boot.

It shook convulsively under the water, but Bob fiercely swam the best he could, willing to resist until his lungs did not give any more of themselves and when he could not take any more, he released his hold and rose to the surface.

He did not see the smuggler again. He didn't know if he had been drowned or washed away by the current, but he hadn't been able to do more to get revenge.

And then his fight for salvation began.

Depleted of faculties, every time he tried to swim cutting off the current he felt drawn by it and could not overcome it. This forced him to continue downstream, appealing to his great swimming skills.

Sometimes he would turn on his back and take care to stay afloat with minimal effort to regain energy, since he would not be able to stay in the water indefinitely. At some point it would have to land or it would sink for good.

And so he went vertiginously away without knowing where the river was taking him, or if he could ever get out of it. I was anxiously trying to see something. Visibility was very poor in the starlight and he had no idea of the landscape. Only shadows cut vaguely in the faint blue glow of the night vaguely passed before his fever-red eyes and he saw no more.

Suddenly, he felt a thump on his feet. He had the feeling that it could be his enemy that had reached him and he was trying to return the tragic play and he turned at the moment when what had hit him spinning in the water, began to slide down one of his flanks. The touch that it produced made him understand that it was a tree carried by the current and he quickly stretched out a hand.

One of the overhanging branches struck him in the arm. Quickly, he grabbed it and held the trunk preventing it from moving forward and maneuvering as best he could, he managed to cling to it and take it as a float.

That relieved him a lot. He was about to faint and that providential tree could be his salvation.

And it was. A little further on the river formed a sharp bend; The current pushed the tree around the bend, and when it hit the ledge, it snagged on something. Bob, without wasting a minute, realizing that he had the land two steps away and could not lose it, released the tree and swam fiercely before the water in the whirlpool hitting the bend dragged him back into its turn.

And he half sank to the bottom, but with work he got out of it and painfully reached the shore.

When he stepped onto dry land, the brutal energies that had kept him in the fight faded; he felt his eyes grow cloudy, his muscles lose rigidity, and his flesh seem to turn into flabby rags.

And taking a few hesitant steps, he fell on his face, being stuck to the ground without sense.

The sun was shining quite high when the warmth that its rays gave it revived him. He came back to life slowly, hardly realizing his situation and it took him work and effort to regain his clarity. When at last he regained all his senses, he began to remember the event detail by detail and his dark and hard face reflected the most painful anguish.

Bad for good, battered, defeated, aching and flaccid, he had been saved. It had been a titanic thing, but he had succeeded; but, what had become of Caro? It was now that she remembered him for the first time since falling into the waves of the Great One.

And the pain crushed him. Caro could not have withstood the attack of his enemy, much less a dive in the Rio Grande in the middle of the night.

And he thought of his mother and sister, of the pain that would beset them when they learned of the tragedy and the responsibility that this death would throw on their shoulders for having been the one who influenced Caro to join the rangers.

As if his body were made of stone, he struggled to his feet. He was drenched in water, exhausted, and his left shoulder ached unbearably, no doubt because he was now swelling more strongly from the blow.

He laboriously approached the river. It glided turbulently and it was not necessary to think that any barge that climbed up it could approach the banks to pick it up, because it was dangerous, but impossible.

He would have to use his own means to move on and get to El Paso when and how he could. But he was so exhausted, he needed to recharge for that walk. The river had carried him a few miles from the city and he did not know how he could get there.

That place was deserted. It was all open grassland and the nearest town must be below he didn't know how far away. His odyssey would be doubly painful, because the length of the march would make him tired, hungry and in pain.

But he couldn't waste time. The more he lost his torment the greater it would be and he had to cut it short.

His only hope was that some Ranger on watch duty along the river would descend far enough to discover him.

And enduring his pains he began to walk slowly towards the north.

The march was difficult. It was almost mid-afternoon when he had exhausted his energies and he felt faint. He couldn't move on and would be forced to flop down on the grass and spend one more night of torment. And when exhausted he collapsed on the ground, he caught the gallop of some horses. As electrified, he stood up and looked for the source of that gallop.

His joy was unspeakable when he discovered that it was a pair of Rangers. When they discovered him, they galloped to meet him.

"Sergeant Reggs, Sergeant Reggs!

"Hello guys, how are you around here?

"Good heavens, how are you, Sergeant! But thank goodness he's at least alive.

"That's right, guys. You won't tell me you were looking for me.

"Of course we were looking for you, Sergeant. There are twenty men walking the river looking for him.

"How did you know it could be around here?

"For his brother Caro.

"Hey? Expensive? Is my brother saved?

"Yes, sergeant. He appeared mid-day in El Paso with a boat and two smugglers whom he had annulled by smashing their heads with a stone. It has been something big according to what they have told us and he was the one who said that they had fallen into the river and that is why we were looking for him here.

Bob, with tears in his eyes, dropped to his knees and thanked heaven for Caro's salvation. Then he begged for water and something to eat, which he devoured with a fierce appetite.

More comforted, he got on one of the horses and asked for details of his brother's odyssey, but no one could give them because they were ignorant of everything that had happened.

And it was already night when they entered the barracks where Captain Walter, gloomy and nervous, was walking through the courtyard dominated by the greatest pessimism about the fate of the sergeant.

His joy was immense when he saw him enter and advancing towards him, he cried out:

"At last, Bob, you have had us with our souls in tow!

"I'm sorry, Captain, I... but please, where is my brother?

The shouting that occurred upon the arrival of the sergeant alarmed Caro, who appeared running in the courtyard. When she saw Bob, she lunged towards him and without being able to speak a word, she hugged him convulsed. Bob felt his eyes fill with tears and stroked her hair, saying;

"How glad I am, Caro! I thought that...

"And me? What I have suffered thinking of you and ours.

"Well, it's all over now. Now stand firm.

The captain, indicating the sheds, ordered;

"Bob, change your clothes and dress up a bit. When you're ready come up to my office; you too, Caro.

Half an hour later the three were reunited in the office, where the two brothers related their adventures to each other separately.

Bob, very proud to learn of Caro's feat, said:

"My captain, I hope you were satisfied with the test. I was sure that my brother would not leave me in a bad place.

"Not. He has been brave, and in due course he will get his reward. Now, what you have to think about is taking advantage of the data captured by Caro and not leaving Harry abandoned. He, too, is in great danger for cooperating with the operation.

"Naturally. Harry also has a ranger mettle and I acknowledge his credit. We have been a bit of a hero by force, but he is being it in cold blood, looking for danger. I hope this helps so that we don't lose contact with him if we locate the crew.

"Have you interrogated that pair of vultures yet?

"Not. One hasn't come to his senses yet and the other, I don't think, will be able to say anything. The doctor finds him very serious and mistrusts that he will be saved.

"One less vulture. As long as the other can speak ...

"Don't trust too much, Sergeant. Most of these men are self-controlled dummies. They know only how little they are told or ordered and Tymson is not going to trust them with explaining his plans. But they will know something, for example, where the gang has, its shelter and perhaps where the contraband is. Something to help you better locate them.

"We will try. Now, the main thing is to see how these people are monitored and located in La Mesa. If Tymson misses the three or four men he has lost in his escape, he will be very on his guard and will vary his plans. I'm not really sure we'll find it in La Mesa, and even less, contraband. I think we still have a lot of bones to gnaw on.

"As long as the bone is close to the teeth, we will gnaw it.

"In that case, you should rest from so much fatigue and recover. Let the doctor look at that shoulder that hurts so much and we will study the plan to follow.

Bob had to lie down and the doctor examined his shoulder. He had no broken bones, but he did have great swelling from the blow.

The brave sergeant slept little and badly that day. The fever seized him and his temperature rose greatly and the doctor predicted that in a week he would not be in a position to be able to serve on active duty.

This was contrary to the captain who wanted to entrust him with the service to be performed. A week was a long time, given the shortage of time.

He was thinking of Caro, but the boy, though brave and tough, lacked experience for certain services and was going to be forced to entrust the mission to another sergeant.

That night he tried to question the wounded smuggler. He persisted in saying that he knew very little about Tymson's business. They had dispatched him to El Paso to take his boss away in the boat when he was ready to leave and he only knew that a week later he would have to concentrate on La Mesa, where he was meeting with his partner.

But the captain besieged him with questions.

Where did the boat come from? "I ask.

"From San Elizondo. There he ordered us to go find him.

"And the one that was left here on the boardwalk when you undocked?

"I don't know of another boat.

"It seems that you do not want to know anything and that is very dangerous. There are some good hemp ropes to loosen the tongue of the forgetful.

"You can hang me, but I can't say more. He ordered us to pick up the boat that a fisherman named Jack was to deliver to us and wait for him from midnight on the boardwalk. Then, we had orders to leave the boat where we picked it up and go to La Mesa.

"How many people does Tymson have at his command?

"I do not know. Sometimes he gathers up to two dozen men and sometimes fewer, as needed. Who knows about that is Morley, his henchman who is the one who gives us orders.

"Where is Morley? The captain asked, remembering that this was the last name he had taken Harry from.

"Who knows? We saw him four days ago when he gave us the order to perform the service and we have not seen him again.

Walter had to give up any further questioning of the wounded man. For the moment, nothing could get out of him more than what had been said, which was very little, but he hoped that when he recovered somewhat from the deep wound that tormented his head, he would be in a position to press him more, even if it was with quite serious threats.

For the time being, given that apparently the cache would not be in a position to pass to Mexico until a week later, it could wait without prejudice to start taking measures to organize the surveillance and the codend.

To do this, he would have to communicate with the rural people of New Mexico to try to coordinate their efforts at the right time.

Chapter VIII

DANGER AFTER DANGER

Harry felt somewhat nervous when at dawn of the day he found himself far from El Paso without being able to leave the slightest trace so that Bob and his men could follow his trail and be aware of what might happen.

He was beginning to fear that his bold trait would be useless, and instead he would be forced to cooperate with the smugglers in the cache if the Rangers somehow missed him. It was going to be a silly danger for him to run, for he guessed that once caught in the gang's meshes, it would not be very easy for him to break it and escape from them and if he succeeded and escaped, his escape would alter all of Tymson's and his plans. his reports obtained in exposure force only served to disorient his companions.

Morley had shown great ability to get him out of El Paso without anyone knowing. This gave him a slight idea of the skill and cunning of the smugglers and how well his boss had organized this productive and dangerous business.

He guessed that the contraband must have a great value given the offer that had been made to him and if so, the measures taken to protect him must also be very harsh and cumbersome.

But there was no longer a choice. He would have to move on, and future events would set the tone for his future attitude.

The horses turned north and about three miles they were joined by another couple.

Morley greeted one of them:

"Everything okay, Jim?

"All good, Morley. We left before dawn and no one saw us leave.

"Go ahead. Our mission in El Paso is over.

The four kept on galloping. Harry guessed that the other rider who hadn't parted his lips and who looked like a cowboy, albeit more defeated, was another new element added to the gang.

And the Ranger wondered how many people they would need for the operation, when they had been forced to capture new elements in that somewhat arbitrary way.

In the middle of the day, they stopped in the solitude of the meadow to prepare lunch. No one spoke, and neither of the two new members of the gang seemed determined to ask any questions.

After the snack, they started off again at a steady gallop, and as night fell, Morley said:

"We have to camp here until dawn. We have two days left for tomorrow and at night we will sleep in our own camp.

Harry did a mental calculation. Supposing that in the two days they left a little more than forty miles behind them and walking somewhat diagonally, it had to be assumed that the lair was in the series, of small mountains that were staggered from south to north until they entered the division of Nuevo Mexico.

Harry's calculations weren't wrong. At dusk the next day, they reached one of these mountains known as Cerro Alto.

It was not very extensive, but it was steep, complicated and, in case of danger, very defensible due to the structure of its crust and its huge crags raised almost to the peak.

They entered a narrow fissure and Morley took the lead. The labyrinth of steps was complicated because they crossed and forked continuously and only he was able to know the route well.

At last they approached two huge crags that almost joined each other, leaving a free space through which a wagon could barely fit through struggling.

As he approached, he emitted modulated whistles that were answered from a height and shortly after, a bad-faced guy, equipped with a double-barreled rifle, came out between some rocks to receive them.

"Hello, Morley" he greeted. And back?

"Yes. Here I bring two new items. Nothing in particular?

"Nothing.

"Did the seines arrived?

"They are coming. We have quite a few gathered, but they are still missing.

"In these days the rest will arrive. And wagons?

"Twelve so far.

"Not bad. The rest will also arrive soon. Where is Frederich?

"In there.

"Go.

They entered the high, narrow fissure and found themselves inside a wide, grassy opening. This was a true camp, where about twenty men roamed the vast space like beasts locked in a huge cage.

At first glance, Harry took in the whole picture. There were some long sheds that must have been destined for the men of the gang and distributed around the perimeter of the ravine, twelve solid large carts, piles of boxes of perfect packaging piled up one on top of the other and on the other side, almost a hundred esparto seines. woven in the form of a wide net.

The Ranger was examining everything carefully and wondered what it all meant. What he had in view must be the stash that had to go to Mexico on a close date, and if that was the case and it was perfectly packed in solid wooden boxes and tightly closed, what was the significance of those seines that Morley was so interested in?

It wouldn't take long to find out, but for now, he was very intrigued.

A tall, stocky, tough-looking, menacing guy advanced to meet Morley.

"Hi Joe, what's up? "I ask.

"Not much for now, Frederich. Here I bring you these two good men. Did any more arrive?

"We have two new ones. They arrived two days ago.

"Well, I think that with these and those that have remained in El Paso, it will not be necessary more. How's that going?

"We have not yet started preparing the seines, waiting for the rest to arrive. As soon as we have all of them, we will open the boxes and prepare everything.

"Very well. I will go tomorrow morning to La Mesa where I will meet with the boss. You have to examine the terrain well on that side to make sure that everything will go well. Surely they do not expect the passage to be made through that site, but, anyway, you have to make sure.

"And the boss?

"Having fun in El Paso.

"No alarm symptoms?

"We have not observed anything, but, anyway, the boss does not trust the least. In due course he will disappear like smoke and be sought out.

Frederich took over the two new smugglers and pointed to a duffel bag in the sheds. Then, he indicated that as long as the work did not start, they could wander as they pleased.

Harry didn't ask any questions and his partner, as mute as he, followed suit.

And so, the brave ranger, found himself stuck in the smugglers' burrow surrounded by danger on all sides and without knowing how he was going to evade it and, above all, how he could be useful to the Corps by doing something that would frustrate the delivery of that formidable stash.

Full of curiosity, he walked through the glen and when he had the opportunity, he approached one of the piles of boxes. He had to clench his teeth to keep from gasping as he realized what was before his eyes.

The boxes bore various signs, all of which pointed in one direction. They were boxes of weapons destined for the war combatants that had not been opened or sent to their destination due to the end of the war.

And he wondered how they could have gotten hold of that arsenal that should have had a rigorous control, since it was government material destined for the soldiers.

If it was stolen, it was not explained how they could take it from the Intendancy warehouses without them realizing it and, if it was not, it had to be admitted that in these warehouses there were allies of the smugglers who facilitated the exit of that material, who knew if feigning a legal destination they would never get to.

The next day, someone notified that two wagons were arriving. A connoisseur of the terrain came looking for them and later they entered the camp. They arrived loaded with empty seines and both the vehicles and the drivers were left in the den.

And the next day, at Frederich's command, he began the work that so intrigued Harry.

It consisted of opening the boxes, unpacking the weapons, and transferring them to the seines, but in a way that could mislead people about their content.

These seines were filled with fresh grass that covered the mesh on the outside and then, skillfully, the interior was filled with weapons placed with art so that they did not appear anywhere. Once the weapons were in place, they were covered with grass and closed solidly. At first glance, they only contained fresh grass to feed livestock.

Harry admired the ploy. No one could suspect wagons loaded with seines that, without a thorough search, only contained feed for cattle.

The simple thing was to have loaded the boxes as they had arrived. Whether the smuggling was to be passed by force or incognito, that work, or those precautions, was not explained, but given Tymson's skill, he guessed something more subtle than what the Rangers assumed. Surely the thing had to be organized in such a way that those carts with that false shipment could pass in front of the noses of those in charge of avoiding it without suspecting what they contained.

Harry worked like the most in the packing and for a few days the operation was carried out calmly but carefully. Frederich watched all the containers and they were not tied until he gave his approval.

Harry had the same companion who had made the journey with him. The Ranger was watching him carefully and seemed to guess that he was not very happy, which made him guess that he had been deceived, or that necessity had forced him to accept something that did not satisfy him.

And he made up his mind to pull his tongue.

"Good job, mate," he commented. If things go well, we are going to pocket enough to give ourselves the great life for some time.

"Yes, this will all be fine if something doesn't happen.

"What's going to happen? Morley has told me that this is done very often and they have never discovered anything.

"Morley will say what he wants, but a few months ago there was a pitched battle on the divide, in which more than ten drivers from a cache like this fell and almost all the cargo ended up in the river.

"Everything has its bankruptcies. Do you think this will also have them?

"I dont know. I would be glad not, but if we go well, I assure you that I will stay in Mexico. I do not like this.

"Why did you come?

"He was drowned, penniless. They told me they gave me a well-paid job and I took it. Later I learned about the work class and there was no longer a choice. If I ever said that I quit, they would not have let me go.

"It's possible. When you commit to something like this, you are already hooked. We trust that everything goes well and we stay in Mexico to follow another course.

"You are not satisfied either?

"A thousand dollars help to settle. I was like you and I needed money.

"It's true. Money forces many things.

They did not comment further. Harry knew enough to, in due course, if he needed to, proceed according to the circumstances. He was sure that if he needed his partner's help, he would have it, especially if he learned of his ranger status.

The packing operation was happily completed within a week and the seines were placed on the carts solidly tied with ropes.

For greater assurance, some of them, especially those that protruded from the rear, contained only grass. It was a measure in anticipation of an attempted registration.

One afternoon, Harry was surprised by the arrival of two horsemen. It was these, Tymson and Morley, coming to examine the cargo and presumably to lead it when they took to the prairie.

Tymson was no longer the smart, well-dressed guy I'd seen at the joint. Now he wore a tacky cowboy outfit, touching his head with a wide stanton hat. His shirt was gaudy, his blue denim pants, high boots and two impressive colts at the waist.

Morley was also dressed in a similar fashion and this made the Ranger suspect that they were about to embark on the final chapter of the adventure.

With his nerves tense, he walked through the glen trying to capture something of what they were talking about between them and Frederick. It was very important to him, because his future attitude could depend on what he found out.

And although it was not much, he did hear something that, at some point, if luck was with him, could be of great use.

It was a loose question from Frederich and an answer from Tymson.

"Where will we cross, boss?

"By Filmore. A lot of feed passes through there to the ranches on the other side of the river. There is a large barge that will cross the wagons. As everything will be done within American territory, nobody can suspect anything. Then we'll talk when we get to the divide.

Harry was puzzled. The plan was well combined, since they were not going to cross the river on the border with Mexico, but to pass to the opposite side within the territory of New Mexico. Later, they would not have the inconvenience of the river to pass to the neighboring State, but a line of land with an illusory border that would not be an obstacle for the running of the carts.

All very well combined and capable of disorienting the rangers who would wait for the stash by the river.

* * *

Meanwhile, in El Paso, Captain Walter had been studying the action of his men. He anticipated that he would need many and had ordered the removal of rangers from different sectors to have them grouped and available at any precise moment.

Bob's condition did not seem to allow him to deal with the case with the necessary energy and he decided to entrust such a mission to another of the most expert sergeants. The latter, with Caro as an assistant, would go to La Mesa to carry out inquiries. The sergeant was ordered to arrest Tymson if he found him in the village.

Caro, for his part, had to carry out espionage dressed in civilian clothes. He was still unknown to the smugglers and this detail could be valuable to him.

And the boy, emboldened by his initial success, had grown enormous and felt capable of the greatest heroics.

Caro got out ahead of Sgt. His mission was exploratory and later, when the sergeant joined him, he would give an account of his discoveries.

But while Caro arrived at La Mesa on time, the sergeant did not, because something unforeseen happened that made him arrive late.

It was all spoiled by the arrival of the sole survivor of the boat the two Rangers had manned. He was the one who fought with Caro and who, despite having received a severe blow to the head with an oar, was able to gain the shore and hide until he crossed the danger line and present himself at La Mesa when Tymson was about to leave the town to join the smuggling and take control of it.

The smuggler appeared with a bandaged head, although he hid it with his hat. Tymson, seeing him, asked:

"What news do you bring, Jules? And your partner?

"My partner? The devil who knows, boss. Something tragic happened after you left and this is the date that I don't know what happened to Carl.

Tymson frowned and exclaimed:

"Speak up, say what happened.

The false fisherman reported the presence of the two rangers in the boat and how they were forced to follow them. Then he recounted the fight and how the boat had capsized throwing everyone into the current.

"I don't know what would happen" he added "; I wanted to capture one of them, but he was able to grab an oar and hit me on the head. This prevented me and I was on the verge of not being able to win the shore. I succeeded and I was able to come here in time to give an account of the event.

Tymson didn't like the news. Of his four men, he was the first to arrive, and the rest must already be there.

"I don't like this," he said, "because if either of them has been saved, they will be trying to find my clue. I supposed they were watching me, but not that much.

«So you are going to stay here in case your companions arrive and send them to the shelter. If the day after tomorrow they haven't returned, take the road and don't worry about them anymore.

And that same night, Tymson, with his second, left La Mesa to get to safety in anticipation of a search by all the towns in the river area.

Caro, unaware of the presence of the guy who had been about to send him to eternity, had stayed at one of the two inns in La Mesa posing as a cowboy returning from vacation. He planned to finish them there by resting for two or three days and then continuing south.

But the same day that the sergeant was supposed to arrive to meet Caro and learn what he might have discovered to deploy the men already prepared to intercept the cache, the unexpected happened. When Caro appeared at the door of the inn with the intention of going out for a walk, since she had not been able to locate anyone, she discovered with infinite amazement a rider who, equipped with a blanket, travel bag and rifle, was leaving the other inn situated a little below hers and apparently embarking on a journey.

His astonishment was tremendous when he recognized the smuggler who was about to finish him off in the river and his first impulse was to go after him to stop him, but taken by an inspiration he was tense seeing him descend the road towards the meadow.

And without wasting a minute he looked for his horse, hastily paid for the inn, and leaping into the saddle he prepared to follow the smuggler at a distance.

He had to go somewhere and if luck favored him and he did not lose sight of him, perhaps it would take him to some place of capital importance for his mission.

Taking all sorts of precautions and relying on his keen eyesight, he followed him at a distance where it was almost impossible to distinguish him. The fact that no other rider was circulating on the plain favored him so as not to mislead him.

Thus he pursued him for hours until, in the evening, they approached a more rugged terrain that would allow him to shorten the distance.

But his fear was that during the night it would get lost and he would never get back on track. This made him nervous and he didn't know what to do.

Nightfall stopped him in pursuit and he wondered furiously what he should try.

Until, recklessly, he decided to proceed with caution. If the smuggler had camped, he might be able to discover him under the protection that that night there were reflections of the distant moon.

And luck was on his side, because in the search, the glow of a bonfire guided him to the smuggler's camp. He had lit a fire to roast some jerky.

Caro, blessing her lucky stars, went to a not far away place and decided to spend the night awake. When the smuggler cleared the field, he could follow his trail as far as it took him.

At dawn, his enemy prepared to leave, but it was something unexpected that his horse whinnied and Caro's answered the whinny.

The smuggler, realizing that he had someone spying on him nearby, fired a rifle, but Caro, realizing that he could no longer keep the incognito, did not want to give facilities to his opponent and from the place that served as an observatory he pulled revolver and fired fast.

The smuggler, vitally hit, could not stay in the saddle and fell to the ground, dropping the rifle.

Caro, like a tiger, jumped out of her hiding place, revolver in hand, and threw herself at the smuggler, applying the barrel of the gun to his head. The wounded man opened his eyes in horror seeing death so close:

"You again! Damn your skeleton!

"Me again, friend, and this one not like that one, because the surprise was mine. Where did you go so lonely?

"To New Mexico.

"You are in New Mexico, didn't you know?

"I meant to Santa Fe.

"That takes a long time, friend. Where is Tymson waiting for you?

"I do not know what you are talking about.

"You know it well. You were meeting at La Mesa with your boss and Morley. You went there to meet him and yesterday you left the village at midmorning. Do you want me to tell you more?

"If you know everything, what do you ask? Let me die in peace.

"No, I won't let you die in peace if you don't speak up first. Listen, I can give you a chance to save yourself if you speak up.

"What possibility?

"You are injured, but not fatally. You can still save yourself if someone helps you. Tell me where Tymson, Morley, the rest of the gang and the smuggling are gathered right now and I'll spare your life. If you don't speak, I will put a bullet in your head, but I warn you one thing: even if you don't speak, we won't take long to know where they are because you've unknowingly put a ranger in the band. As you will appreciate, if you do not speak, you do not advance anything or save yourself, or save others. The band is going to be cool and if they caught you there you would be shot or hanged.

The smuggler hesitated a moment and replied:

"If you heal me as best you can to hold out until they pick me up, I'll tell you.

"Done deal. Waiting.

He searched the travel bag for the healing supplies Rangers always carried for emergencies and uncovered the wound. He had a bullet in the chest that was bleeding outrageously.

With water from the wineskin, he washed the injury, made a plug of lint soaked in iodine, and inserted it into the wound, making the smuggler scream with pain. Then she applied a compress to him and left him lying on the grass.

"You are there and I can't do better. Now talk.

"Tymson is reunited with his gang and the smuggling on a hill about fourteen miles from here called Cerro Alto. This is where everyone is getting ready to take out the stash.

"They are many?

"A couple dozen.

"In what direction is that?

"Going straight ahead. There is no other hill near it.

Caro asked no more. He was interested in discovering the hill, locating it, if it was possible to approach it and verify that the wounded man had not lied and then, with all the possible data, gallop to El Paso, tell Walter about his discovery and present himself there with three dozen hardened men. Rangers to storm the bush and not let a single smuggler escape.

He left the wounded man's horse locked and mounted on his own, he went away in the direction of the mountain.

Slowly he approached the designated place until in the distance he discovered the upright silhouette of Cerro Alto isolated on the plain.

He stopped hesitantly. If he approached in broad daylight, he was in serious danger of being discovered.

The best thing he could do was to camp right there, wait patiently for the day to come to an end and when the night came under the cover of shadows, approach the mountain, filter through one of its fissures and search for Tymson's crew until they located it. Then, once certain they were in the bush, he could retreat before the sun shone again and at full gallop, busting his horse if necessary, reach El Paso and report his discovery to the captain.

And controlling his nerves he got off his horse and prepared to wait patiently for the empire of the shadows.

Chapter IX

ON THE VERGE OF DEATH

The silver-lit stars began to glow as shadows fell over the moor.

Caro set out to carry out her plan. He was afraid that hours later the moon would rise, illuminating the landscape and making his work more difficult and he had to hurry if he did not want to fail when success was at hand.

He slowly gained ground and approached the mountain. He believed that it was very difficult that with the reigning gloom they could discover him and when he found himself in the foothills of the rocky massif he locked his horse in a place that would allow him to reach him soon and boldly decided to get into that unknown plot.

He trusted his courage, his prudence and the very little clarity that prevailed. Everything would protect him and help him to crown his plan.

Introducing himself through some cuts that he found nearby, he began to ascend in search of possible refuge. The silence was impressive and nothing denounced that he could be near the lair, He advanced painfully, having to choose between the many forks that were presented to him as he advanced, but his sense of direction led him to choose the ones that went deeper deep into the mountain and not those that made him drift to its flanks.

From time to time, he would stop, listen eagerly, and go on a bit bewildered, fearing that later he would have trouble finding his way out of this mysterious labyrinth.

He had been feeling the ground for half an hour, when one of the times when he listened he thought he caught on his right a murmur of voices and some horse neighing and shuddering with joy, he tried to orient himself to get to the place that seemed to him the object of his anxieties .

As he progressed, his suspicions grew. He hadn't been wrong; not far away there must have been a concentration of people who carelessly in their refuge did not take precautions not to be discovered.

"And I advanced until I reached the two high crags that gave the entrance to the refuge.

Joyful, he threw himself to the ground and crawling like a lizard continued to advance. He wanted to peek through that narrow fissure and, if possible, have a look around the camp; then, when he was sure of his discovery, he would retreat, seek the exit from the mount, and gallop to El Paso to report everything to the captain.

But suddenly, when he was crawling on the stone, something heavy and violent fell on him as if it had detached from the top of the rock and when he wanted to realize what it was, they had applied a hard blow to the head and two hands iron squeezed his throat until he was suffocated.

And in the anxiety of that tragic situation he caught a strange hiss and a voice that shouted:

"Jackson, Jackson! Come here help me, I have hunted something very interesting.

Immediately, new hands gripped him, someone snatched the revolver from him and, lifting him to his feet, they took him by the arms like a wimp.

"Well, little friend, the curiosities are paid and yours will have its prize.

They penetrated the fissure and Jackson sounded an alarm. Soon after, Tymson, Morley, and Frederich appeared in alarm.

"What's going on? Asked the first of the three.

"This lizard that crawled up the rock pretending to stick its nose in here.

Tymson clenched his teeth angrily. The presence of the intruder was very alarming, because, even if it was only one, it indicated that they were on his heels in a moment as crucial as this one.

And, furious, he ordered:

"Take him to the bonfire; I want to see his face.

Caro, half asphyxiated, a trickle of blood flowing from the wound that had caused the blow to his forehead, was pushed towards a bonfire. All the smugglers, tense, ran towards it possessed of nervous curiosity to know who the intruder was.

Harry, along with the cowboy who had joined him in the gang at the same time and with whom he had become close friends in case he was interested in their friendship at some point, came forward fearful of what might happen. He took it for granted that only a Ranger could be so daring that he would defy danger by committing that act of bravery.

But her astonishment was tragic when, looking at him, she recognized Caro in him. A shudder of anguish shook her body and she thought she fell to the ground. Instinctively he had to grab onto his partner's arm to keep himself upright.

The cowboy noticed and, looking at him, asked in a low voice:

"What's the matter with you, Harry? Do you ... know him?

"Yes, and I would give my life if it served to save yours.

"Who is it? Any ranger?

Harry nodded.

"How do you know him?

"It's that I treat her mother and her sister, a very pretty and very good girl.

"Yeah, you like the girl. Why then ...?

"Hush, don't talk now. Is better.

Tymson, reflecting on his hard face all the rage and cruelty of which he was capable, ordered Morley:

"Register him from top to bottom.

Caro, after the first moment of panic, was redone. He realized the end that awaited him And in a courageous reaction he wanted to show that he was a man who knew how to win and lose and who would not show himself a coward at the time of his death.

And remembering Harry, she anxiously sought him out. If he was there, as he expected, he wanted him to realize what kind of man he was, and if he was saved, he wanted him to witness how he had done his duty until the last moment, honoring the Corps he belonged to.

When she discovered him and their eyes crossed like swords, they both remained tense, but neither betrayed themselves by denouncing their knowledge.

Suddenly Morley, triumphant, showed something, saying:

"I figured it was, boss. Look this.

"Already; with a ranger badge. Well, buddy, you are not the first curious to poke your nose in my affairs and go to hell without indulging in finishing your work. Let's see what you have to tell us.

And Caro, in a fit of pride, bellowed:

"Simply, that you are indecent pigs who are trading with the lives of many men. Yes, I am a Ranger, I declare it with pride and I do not mind dying in the line of duty because I know that behind me there are many others to avenge my death. It will not take long for them to turn and when we meet in hell we will talk about this matter.

Tymson stepped forward and slapping him fiercely, cried out:

"We won't see you there for a long time, you filthy tracker, because I'm worth too much so no one can cut me off. Where are the others? Speak up or I'll tear you apart.

"It's the same to me, I don't know, but if I knew I wouldn't say it. I have come here by chance, because I have surprised one of the guys who manned the boat in which they tried to drown us in the river and I have overwhelmed him, forcing him to speak.

«I came to make sure that his accusation was true and if I have failed, worse for me, not for that reason there will be someone luckier than me, and if he is going to celebrate my death as something extraordinary, I will embitter his success by telling him something he does not know; I am already avenged in advance because of the four who manned the two boats, none will ever repeat the feat or smuggle.

«Those who took you to the riverbank did not leave the pool with the boat, because I loaded them and of the two who manned the boat where we foolishly embarked my brother and I do not live. One drowned in the river and I surprised the one that remained in La Mesa and followed him until I finished with him. Now you can kill me whenever you want, but think about what a single ranger has been able to do. Later on, the others will show you many things because that stash ... that stash will never pass to Mexico.

A general clamor welcomed Caro's brave statement. Harry was scared of his courage and his partner looked at him in amazement.

Tymson, holding back his rage, bellowed:

"Be quiet. Look for this guy's horse that will be left somewhere. You have to take care that there are no traces of its presence and when you find it, bring it.

Then he added, indicating to Morley:

"When the horse is brought in, I will give you more orders.

And he began to walk like a rabid wolf through the ravine, while two smugglers went out to look for the horse.

Harry was devastated, realizing that there was no human power to save Caro. She had gone too far in trying something beyond her strength and she was going to pay for it with her life without him being able to do anything in her favor.

The cowboy, whose name was Ruffus, tugged on Harry's arm and exclaimed hoarsely:

"Did you hear what he said? That the contraband will not reach Mexico. Do you think it will be like this?

And Harry, gambling everything on one card, replied:

"Not only do I believe it, but I know it.

"How?

"Listen to me, Ruffus. I know that you are sorry for having come and I feel sorry for the fate of others. It is still time for you to save yourself if you want.

"How?

"That ranger is not the only one hot on the heels of the gang. There are several other invisible ones around her, and I am one of them. I am going to be in great danger, but when the time comes for the fight I can save you if you stand by my side. Tymson is stuck in a fence that he senses, but ignores, and whether or not he kills that unfortunate, his end is near.

Now answer. You can also denounce me and they will kill me with it, but when it comes to beating the gang you will fall with everyone. If, on the other hand, you are willing to help me when necessary, you will save yourself because I will be the one who supports you so that no one includes you on the list of undesirables.

Ruffus, with a sincere accent, replied:

"I don't know what will happen, Harry, but I swear to you that I will be by your side in everything. If I am to die, I prefer to do it with dignity.

"Thanks. I hope we have a bit more luck than that brave man.

An hour later, the two ruffians appeared with Caro's horse.

Tymson returned to his prisoner, and indicated:

"Very well. Tie him up well, mount him on the horse and take him to the Devil's Plateau. It is an ideal place with a good chasm at the foot that does not return its dead. Take away "he told Morley" three men and when he is at the top with a couple of shots to the horse and the man you will send them to the chasm. It is cleaner and leaves no trace.

Morley smiled and turned his head. Those closest to him were Harry, Ruffus, and one other.

Harry trembled as if a powder keg had exploded in his veins. If he lacked something to make his situation more amazing, it had to be the executioner of his unfortunate companion.

And a red veil of blood crossed his eyes. Rather than firing a single shot at Caro, he preferred to get riddled with it.

Ruffus, too, was distraught as he understood his companion's pain.

But he reacted quickly and prepared to accompany Morley and the prisoner.

Caro was handcuffed, put on the horse and locked his legs under the belly of the poor animal.

Morley took the horse by the bridle and the three designated as the execution picket followed.

Harry, who was not resigned to seeing Caro die, worked his brain in search of a desperate solution and followed Morley along with Ruffus while the other smuggler stood by the horse's side, in case the rider lost his grip. Balance.

Suddenly, Harry put his head close to Ruffus's ear and said:

"We have to save that boy.

"How? The frightened cowboy hissed.

"Listen to me. When we get to the rock and when those two vultures are distracted, we will shoot them from point of shot eliminating them. Then we will release Caro so she can escape and gallop in search of the rangers. They will be here soon and this will be over.

"And we?

"We can hide in some defensible place from which it would not be difficult for us to hold off whoever was looking for us and trying to hunt us down. We will spend a few hard hours, but choosing the site well we will stay until the rangers arrive. It is a very viable project and I swear to you that you will not lose anything if you second it.

The cowboy was silent for a while as they walked away in search of the tragic plateau. Harry was looking at him with aching longing waiting for his answer.

And the cowboy, with a nod, nodded.

Harry felt his hopes revive. The project was dangerous, but there was no other.

Climbing up rough paths they moved away from the lair until they reached a great height, the base of which was flat and not of very wide dimensions.

When they reached it, Harry realized its structure. On the other side it was cut vertically and sank to an incalculable depth.

The moonlight bathed the fateful rock gloomily, and Morley, releasing his horse, indicated:

"You do not know this do you? Well, look out. This guy will find a skeleton down there that will welcome him so he won't feel so alone. Behold!

He walked over to the edge along with the other smuggler.

Harry quickly conceived a new, simpler project and with a gesture expressed it to Ruffus. Then he came forward and when he reached Morley who was looking down, with a brutal push he lost his balance and threw him into the void.

An impressive scream tore the silence. The other undesirable wanted to turn, but Ruffus, imitating his partner, did not give him time and also threw him into the void.

And then, there was an agonizing silence that Ruffus broke, saying:

"Done, Harry. What comes next, may be pointed out by destiny.

Harry took her hand and assured:

"Ruffus, my life ahead of yours if I must die. What you have done will pay off.

He ran to the horse, untied Caro's bonds, who had almost fainted with emotion.

"Quick, Caro, get out of the bush and look for our companions. Fly as much as you can or success will not be complete.

But the boy, excited, cried out:

"Harry, what you have done for me and your partner is also something I will never forget, but you have put yourselves in danger for me and I cannot escape it. I'll stay with you and ...

"Enough," Harry bellowed. You will leave right now or this will have been useless. Leave us, we know what we have to do. We will resist through the rocks until your arrival. Do not delay or you will be the culprit that everything goes wrong.

Caro didn't dare to protest. He shook hands with both of them and at an indication from Harry he chose the descent path out of the bush before they missed the others and could hunt him down.

And when the brave boy disappeared down the hill, Harry indicated:

"And now follow me, Ruffus. We will move away as much as we can while they do not discover what happened and the higher we climb, the better we will defend ourselves and the better we will cover the landscape when my companions arrive. I'm very happy because I think this is going to be the final fight.

And followed by Ruffus, they began to scale heights, ascending and moving as far as possible from the lair.

In this they hoped to catch the detonations. Although the plateau was a little out of the way, the shots could get there and everyone was waiting, eagerly.

More than half an hour passed, until Tymson, indignantly bellowed:

"What the hell are those assholes doing? They should be back by now.

And Frederich, restless, growled:

"I'm going to see what happens; I do not like this.

He hurried to the rock, but when he reached the top he did not discover traces of the five men who had left the lair half an hour earlier and possessed of a tragic presentiment he returned swiftly, shouting:

"Boss, no one can be seen.

"What are you saying?

"That there is no trace of men or horses. I do not explain this.

Tymson lost his temper at the statement and lunged toward the rock, followed by some of his men. But the record was in vain. It seemed as if the chasm had swallowed them all.

And furious, he began to give orders:

"This can not be. Something has happened and serious. Search everywhere until you find one. Two who ride horses and go down to the plain to see if they discover anything. I am fearing many things and by hell that is already too much.

And while two rode on horseback and descended down the mountain, the rest scattered through the accidents of the land looking for the five disappeared.

But his efforts were in vain. The night was not helping either and they were threatened to lose it in a useless search, at least until sunrise.

Chapter X

THE END OF THE FEAT

Overjoyed at the unexpected end of her tragic adventure, Caro galloped like a spear favored by the full light of the glowing moon. His desire was to get to El Paso as soon as possible to give an account of his odyssey and enlist the help of all available rangers. The brave Harry was in a very dangerous situation because of him and he had to reciprocate with him in the same way.

The day was long and exhausting and at dawn the horse showed brutal fatigue threatening to collapse.

And when he stroked his hair in despair, two horsemen crossed the landscape. They were the foreman of a ranch and a laborer on their way to his ranch.

Caro wasted no time. He made himself known, explained the situation and asked to borrow one of the horses, keeping his. The foreman agreed to the change and Caro continued her exhausting journey.

When he arrived in El Paso, exhausted, blood pouring from his head wound and with the sign of the brutal blow that Tymson had administered to him, he had almost no strength to recount his odyssey. Captain Walter listened to him with tense nerves and then asked:

"You say that the mountain is called Cerro Alto?

"That is the name they gave me.

"Well. Retire and rest. I know where it is and I don't need your contest. You would stay in the middle of the road and your effort would be of no use. You have exhausted your energies and you are fine.

Caro hardly heard him; he was falling asleep sitting in the chair.

The captain put him to bed and quickly began calling men. He gave them a quarter of an hour to be mounted and equipped for the march.

Bob, almost recovered, wanted to join the game. Harry's feat of saving his brother's life when he was hopelessly lost demanded equal compensation and he was willing to sacrifice his own in order to save Harry.

Forty men made up the squad. Captain Walter was willing not to make concessions to the enemy but to destroy him forever and was in the vanguard to direct the operation in person.

With periodic stops of an hour to regain strength and give the horses a margin of rest, they rode all day and all night. That system of stops allowed a greater effort in the advance, although all accused the sleep and the fatigue.

And it was midday when they gave a view of the Cerro Alto where the fight was to end.

The plain was deserted, and this indicated that if Tymson's gang had not fled, they must be secluded in the bush.

And there it was, because the smuggler chief, after calculating the pros and cons, had decided not to go out on the plain. If there were some possibilities of defense, and if it was successful, it was there, between the rocks, where they could be defended inch by inch.

The bad thing for him was that in an unexpected way he had lost eight men from his crew and this was going to be very noticeable at the time of the fight.

When the rural people approached the mountain, the roar of intense gunfire reached their ears, echoing through the hollows of the mountain. After an anxious search they had managed to locate Harry and his companion and had put all their courage in hunting them down, guessing that their treachery had set the prisoner free, disposing of Morley and his companion.

But the two braves had found a difficult height to climb and had become strong on it. Protected by the rocky overhangs of the crag, they shot everyone who approached and tried to put them in range or climb to the top, and they had already knocked out two other smugglers.

But they were under siege, without food, without water, and with nothing to put in their mouths. They were forty-eight hours of deadly anguish defending themselves like wild beasts and taking turns in surveillance during the night so as not to be surprised.

Both had dry mouths as esparto grass and hunger plagued them, but they continued to fight fiercely and skimp on the lead. Their opponents tried to force them to deplete their reserves and then have them at their mercy, but both only fired when they were in danger or when they thought someone was within range of their shots.

Ruffus seemed desperate that they would arrive in time to save them, but Harry was cheering him on. He was sure that the day would not end without the Rangers showing up.

And he was not wrong. Shortly before midafternoon from his height, Harry discovered a compact mass that was advancing between clouds of dust and excited, he exclaimed:

"Ruffus, attention! The rangers!

The cowboy looked out over the plain with reddened eyes and shuddered. The wave of dust rushed forward in a wide swath.

How many will come, Harry?

"Enough, don't worry, mate.

A deafening shout broke out from among the boulders. The smugglers had just discovered their centuries-old enemies, and confusion had taken hold of them.

Tymson, furious to the point of paroxysm, began issuing orders like mad. All the entrances to the mountain had to be blocked to prevent the Rangers from entering it.

This forced them to ignore Harry and his partner. The danger was elsewhere and the two besieged did not seem to worry them.

But he did take care to leave a man in ambush to prevent them from leaving his shelter and becoming a wedge to his back. They had to immobilize them there while the others faced the squad of uniforms.

Soon they were at the foot of the mountain, spreading throughout to offer the smallest target and at the same time disunite the enemy forces and be able to attack them more easily.

Their tired horses galloped from side to side while the excellent rifles of the scouts fired against the cliffs where they glimpsed the silhouette of some smuggler, or caught the detonation of their weapons.

When the fight became general, Harry, who did not want to remain idle, invited his partner:

"Shall we go down? I think that at the rear we can be very useful.

"Whatever, in order to end this ordeal" roared the cowboy, maddened by thirst, above all.

Harry was the first to attempt the descent. He leaned out and looked down without seeing anyone. Then he began to descend carefully.

And when he was in the middle of the slope, a detonation vibrated from a rock. Harry felt the ember of the bullet brush against his side and he roared in pain, but swiftly, he fired when he discovered a head poking out to catch the effect of his shot.

The smuggler was struck down by the bullet that had entered his skull and there were no more shots fired at them.

Harry continued to descend uncomfortably. The bullet had ripped through his side and he felt the searing brush as he moved, but hard as steel, he was not about to be relegated to passivity.

Both reached the foot of the rock and Ruffus, realizing the state of his companion, was scared:

"What was that, Harry?

"Nothing important, Ruffus. A scratch Go ahead, there is something more urgent to do.

And applying the handkerchief to the wound underneath his clothes, he tightened his belt to support it.

And laboriously he continued forward with his revolver in hand, guiding himself by the roar of the shots to approach the place where the smugglers were defending the entrance to the mountain.

But the Rangers' tactic and their greater numbers were catching on. Tymson's men, in their attempt to cut off all passage inside, had been forced to open too wide, losing contact, and this forced them to fight one against two and sometimes against three.

And so some Rangers, fortunately, after eliminating the obstacle that opposed them head-on, had managed to penetrate some fissures, while others were still struggling to break through the rest of the defenses.

Soon panic spread. There were rangers inside the bush. They had hunted two from behind and the others, without knowing what to do, were retreating looking for new positions. They had already suffered some casualties and their fighting power was diminishing.

Harry and his partner walked up the back. They soon made contact with a retreating one and knocked him down before he had time to guard against the new danger and the fence tightened dangerously for outlaws.

Tymson, who had fought valiantly as the bravest of his men, realized that all was lost and decided to try a daring maneuver to escape if possible.

He looked for his horse and through the pine trees, paths of rock, he threw it towards the foot of the mountain looking for the exit. If he managed to break the fence, he would have been saved, and if not, he would not fall meekly there locked up.

He was descending a path in a semicircle, when Harry, who had gained the height of some rocks to better encompass the landscape, saw him galloping below him skirting the rock looking for escape and fearful that in his daring he would succeed, he tried to catch up with him. shooting. But his revolver jammed and in despair he had to give up hunting.

But suddenly, in a brutal reaction he ran to the other side of the boulder and looked down. Tymson circled the cliff and would soon pass under it.

And without hesitation, he waited. Then he flinched, leaped, and fell on top of the smuggler as he crossed below him.

They both rolled like a strange ball falling from the horse. The frightened animal continued to gallop alone and the two enemies, in a mortal embrace, struggled for a moment on the stone of the narrow path.

But Harry, who had the advantage of having fallen on top, managed to grab the bandit by the neck and when he tried to shake him off with his knees, digging them brutally into his chest, and causing the pain in his side even more, he shook his head fiercely. convulsive movements and the smuggler's skull smashed into the stone of the trail in a dull, mind-boggling roll, until it was limp in the Ranger's hands.

He stood up hesitantly with cloudy eyesight, his temples burning and a huge noise inside his head, and collapsed like a doll when Ruffus came to his aid.

Meanwhile, the battle was subsiding. More than half of the smugglers had fallen, other wounded were defending themselves savagely and some were trying to escape into the fissures of the forest pursued by the Rangers who were not willing to let just one flee.

Bob and Captain Walter were eagerly looking for Harry, fearing for his life, since according to Caro, he had left him with someone who helped him at the mercy of the bandits.

At last Bob, searching, entered the path where Tymson and Harry had just fallen. Ruffus, next to him, leaned over the ranger trying to help him, as his first impression was to believe that he had fallen dead from some wound received in the fight.

The sergeant, when facing the group, extended his arm, presenting the revolver, while ordering:

"Hands up!

Ruffus was quick to obey, yelling:

"Don't shoot, Sergeant. I'm the one who helped Harry save the prisoner and ...

Bob lowered his arm and, stepping ahead of the cowboy, offered his hand, saying:

"Are you the one who helped Harry to throw those who were going to kill my brother Caro into the chasm?

"His brother? Well yeah, it's me ... He can attest to it when he comes to, and that ... that's Tymson, the crew chief. Harry caught him by jumping from up there on him when he tried to escape on horseback. I warn you that you are injured. We were shot at the last minute when we descended from the shelter where we have been staying since his brother escaped from here.

Bob called a ranger who was shooting next to him and between the three of them they lifted Harry's body to get him out of there. They did not know his state of gravity, but everything had to be done for him.

Little by little, the battle diminished. Loose shots rang out inside; They were rangers who were chasing the last survivors and the rangers were beginning to gather around their captain.

Word soon spread that Harry had been found and Walter rushed to meet him. Bob introduced him to the cowboy who had contributed so much to the success of the company, and the brave ranger was taken out of the bush and placed on the grass to proceed with an emergency treatment.

Meanwhile the captain, approaching Ruffus, exclaimed:

"You will tell me everything, but for now I am interested in knowing what happened to the contraband.

"Follow me and I will take you where you are prepared to be taken out of here and transferred to Mexico. The idea was to pass it off as cattle feed and introduce it into the neighboring country, not through the river, but through the New Mexico divide.

He took them to the lair and showed them the smashed boxes and the seines loaded onto the wagons.

"Very ingenious," said the captain, "and it may not be the first time that weapons have been passed through this procedure. As for smuggling, it will be very curious to investigate how these boxes came out of the Intendancy warehouses. That, the military authorities will have to find out in due course.

After verifying that the cache had not left there, the immediate task was to clean the hill of dejected elements. There were a dozen dead, several wounded, and two prisoners.

Two Rangers also had minor injuries and were treated by their companions just as Harry had been treated.

While this operation was being carried out, the captain interrogated Ruffus. He was intrigued by her presence there and her help to Harry.

The cowboy told how they had tricked him and how he became friends with Harry, who ended up revealing his ranger status and promising to help him avoid being treated like smugglers. He had done his best and thanks to this, Caro had been able to save herself and warn them so that they would arrive in time to save them from the siege and be able to intervene in the cache.

The captain, after hearing the story, said:

"Very good boy, you have behaved decently and bravely and deserve a reward. Would you be interested in joining my Division?

"How? I ranger?

"If you are interested, you are admitted from now on. You have made enough merits for your income.

"Oh, of course I do! I was out of work, and I especially like this, having by my side such brave and determined men as Harry and the Sergeant's brother.

"Well, nothing more, Ruffus. From this moment you are one more in the Body.

The night fell on them and they had to camp in the smugglers' lair, where they found everything they needed to support themselves, as they were well stocked.

Ruffus slept like a dormouse taking revenge for the previous vigilances and the next morning, everything was organized to clean the hill of corpses and remove the contraband from there.

As it was packed, it was moved to the meadow. The wounded were accommodated in a bed of seines and blankets and the dead and prisoners were accommodated in a cart for transfer to El Paso.

And the huge caravan began to move.

* * *

When they reached El Paso, Caro, who had recovered from her exhaustion, looked forward to the return of her companions. He feared for the lives of the two brave men who had risked so much to save him.

When at last he saw them arrive, he ran to meet his brother, asking eagerly:

"Bob, and Harry?

"Don't worry, it comes in a wagon. They hit him on the side, but it's nothing serious.

"And the other one, the one who helped him?

"He also comes with us. The captain has admitted you to the Corps.

"I'm glad; he has been a brave man. Now what are we going to do with Harry?

"Well, heal him, what are we going to do?

"Bob, we should take him home. I would be better cared for there and mother and Cynthia want to see you to thank you for what you did for me.

"Very good, Caro. I will propose to the captain.

* * *

Harry was transferred to the cabin where a bed was set up for him and where the doctor went to treat him and Cynthia went out of her way to take care of him.

The wounded man was under the effects of fever for two days, until it began to subside and the brave ranger realized the reality.

He was overwhelmed when Caro's mother and young Cynthia vehemently expressed their appreciation for his heroism in saving Caro's life. He excused himself by saying that it had all been the work of the line of duty and that it did not matter.

He was very happy when they told him that the gang had been exterminated and that Ruffus was becoming one more ranger in the Corps.

"I'm glad" he exclaimed "; he more than earned it.

For three days he didn't see any of the Reggs, but he didn't miss them. The pleasant company of Cynthia was enough for him, who harassed him with questions and did nothing but ask her for details of his entire odyssey.

On the third day, he was surprised to see the captain, Bob, and Caro arrive. This one did not fit in the uniform on whose sleeve he wore the cape stripes.

Harry, seeing them, smiled and said:

"Congratulations, Caro. You have deserved it.

And the captain, intervened to say:

"Indeed, Sergeant Harry, you have deserved it. I personally come to inform you that you have been praised in the order of the day and that the Chief of the Division has decided to recognize your rank in the Army in the Corps. From this moment on, you are the rangers sergeant. Harry Parker.

Thank you, my captain. I was determined to do my best to earn it and I am proud to have achieved it, because I always believed that I was born to ranger. I no longer wish that new opportunities will present me to endorse my promotion and to be useful to the Corps as far as my strength can reach.

"Very good, Sergeant Harry. Now to recover and when the doctor discharges him, he will obtain a fifteen-day leave for his convalescence. The day has been very hard and he deserves that rest.

I can see that you are pampered here like a child and I celebrate it, because after all, you have contributed to maintaining the happiness of this good family. Let the streak continue.

And he said it with a smile and an expressive wink, which made Cynthia blush and disturbed the wounded man quite a bit. From that moment on, Harry began to recover quickly and soon got up from his bed and spent the hours sitting in the sun at the door of the cabin, being accompanied by Cynthia, who felt possessed of an enormous dynamism, due to the presence of the ranger.

One day Harry said sadly:

"Cynthia, I am very sorry to tell you that I am restored and that I will soon have to rejoin the Division.

"And you regret being restored?

"Yes, because now I will be forced to leave here and not have her by my side constantly.

"But you can come when your occupations allow you.

"Yes, of course, I would very much like it.

"Is someone stopping you?

"No, of course, but I would like something else.

"The fact that?

"That you authorize me to come as more than a patient and a friend.

"How then?

"Didn't you understand me? I like you very much, Cynthia, and I am convinced that my happiness will be complete if I join my promotion with the hope that one day I can aspire to be a member of the family. If fate brought us together spiritually, in a tight bond of camaraderie and adventure, would it be too much to ambition that bond that would bind us more closely? I do not know if I have any merit to aspire to it and I wish it would disappoint me or give me some hope. If I succeeded, I would consider myself the happiest man on earth.

And Cynthia, lowering her head, murmured:

"Harry, you deserve that and more. It has saved my brother's life and it has made us very happy with it; Why not return happiness with happiness if at the same time I can also aspire to be the happiest of women?

Harry took her hand and shook it with emotion and silence. He felt so blissful that he couldn't find words to express his happiness.

END